# SOULS ISLAND

Ann Monné

Order this book online at www.trafford.com
or email orders@trafford.com

Most Trafford titles are also available at major online book retailers.



Print information available on the last page.

ISBN: 978-1-4907-9400-6 (sc)
ISBN: 978-1-4907-9401-3 (e)



*Trafford rev. 02/27/2019*

**North America & international**
toll-free: 1 888 232 4444 (USA & Canada)
fax: 812 355 4082

To
my family
and dear Doreen ('D')
and my good friend Atie

# Contents

# SOULS ISLAND

Emilie Nielson known as Kia, could not remember a great deal about the last weeks. Perhaps she did not want to remember too much about the bright sunny day when Lars died. She had made him breakfast and he had worked for a while on his model sailboat before announcing he was going fishing.

'You promised to clear out the shed and do some weeding,' she had shouted. 'You only think of yourself, Lars. You're a lazy bastard.'

He had filled a thermos flask with coffee, picked up his fishing tackle and given her a peck on the cheek. 'I'll be back in a couple of hours,' he promised as he walked towards the lake, impervious to her anger.

'Do whatever you want. You always do,' she shouted. 'Your only interest is 'me, myself and I'. That is what you are selfish and you are not about to change, not now, not at your age.'

She had done the necessary housework, made herself a mug of coffee, and stared out of the kitchen window expecting to see him sitting, with exaggerated patience, for a fish to snap at his hook but he was nowhere in sight. It had not worried her, perhaps he had walked along the beach; perhaps he had gone to a neighbour. He would be back soon, so she had thought.

Later, she had walked to the end of the jetty only to find his fold-up stool. The box of hooks, bait and their small sailboat were gone. She had squinted across the still water for as far as she could see but there was no sign of him, or any other sailor or windsurfer for that matter, and she had returned to the house even more irritated than she had been earlier that morning.

At the end of the afternoon, she had rung their nearest neighbour, Jens, who lived further down the lake. She had told him how Lars had gone fishing in the morning and had not returned. Jens had told her not to worry and had offered to take his motorboat out and they would look around the small islands where Lars often fished.

They found him on the far side of one of the tiny islets, slumped in the bottom of the boat. His fishing tackle, empty thermos flask and a plastic cup laid next to him; his rod floated in the water with the line curled around an oarlock. He had died of a heart attack.

She would have done anything to relive that morning, not to have shouted at his lack of interest in either house or garden. She wished she had not told him what she thought, wished she had accepted things as they were, accepted him as he was. She would never forgive herself, she felt as though she had killed him. If only she could relive that morning. If only she had kissed him fondly goodbye, if only.

*

It was more than two weeks later when she sat opposite her solicitor, Axel Hansson. She noticed how he had aged as he turned the pages of Lars' testament with trembling hands.

'As you must already know,' he said, reading the print closely, in spite of his gold rim glasses balanced on the end of his nose. 'Lars left everything to you except for a few minor donations to local charities. There are, of course, the rented properties,' he added, turning the page.

'Are they profitable?'

'They are mostly shops and apartments in town centres. They bring in a moderate income. There are no mortgages on any of them and, of course, they constitute a real estate investment. He paused as though to carefully select his words. 'As you must know,' he repeated. 'Lars rented most of the properties to people with problems who don't fall under the social services. He was very socially orientated. He even refused an honour from the Mayor. Said he did not want any publicity. Do you want to keep them?'

'I'll think about it.'

'Let me see,' he answered, as he ran his bony finger down a list. 'One lease has just been terminated. Lars did that the day before he died. It is a one man business, photograph shop, I believe.'

'He must have had a reason to do that.'

'He must have. Anyway, he seemed determined so I did what he asked. Perhaps he was intending to sell the properties as the leases expired, simplify his estate. Anyway, you do not have to make any decisions now. I will contact you when the leases come up for renewal.'

*

She had been surprised when a few days later she opened her front door to a young girl. Her blond hair fell loosely down the sides of her face, her deep blue eyes and her pale skin completed her beauty.

She had invited her in after she, Lara Lindberg, had told her she had known Lars. They had sat at the kitchen table while she listened to how Lara missed her husband, his company, his kindness. She really did not know what this young girl expected her to say except, perhaps, words of sympathy. How simple could this young thing be or, more likely, how dangerous!

'Why are you telling me this?' she had asked, calmly.

The girl looked down. 'Because I gave Lars something and I would like to have it back.'

'What something would that be, Lara?'

'An old coin. There was a dreadful storm at sea and my grandfather rescued the crew of a fishing boat. The local people clubbed together and gave him an old coin, a collector's coin, in recognition of his bravery.

My grandmother gave it to me before she died. Both my parents died young,' she added, sadly.

'I'm sorry to hear that,' she sympathised. 'But why did you give it to Lars?'

'We got around to discussing old coins. He told me how he once had a few Ducats but he sold them. Then I told him about my grandfather's coin which I always kept in a locket around my neck.' She opened a rather large empty locket. 'I showed it to him and he said he would look it up in a book he had about coins. So I gave it to him.'

'Well, I know nothing of it. He didn't say anything to me about it,' she muttered. 'I will have to look for it. I haven't seen it'.

'I know where it is, Lars told me. He said he would put it in a box of foreign coins for safekeeping. Small change that he had over from trips and holidays abroad.'

'How clever of him. Where did you meet him?' she asked, curiously.

'On one of the islands. I windsurf whenever I can. Lars fished while I watched.'

'That must have been cosy,' she muttered, as she walked over to an antique kitchen dresser. 'How do you know where I live?' she asked, after tipping the contents of a box onto the kitchen table.

'Lars pointed to a group of trees on the other side of the lake and said his house was between them.'

'Really,' she murmured, with a hint of sarcasm as Lara spread the coins over the table and, without any hesitation, picked up a dull coin which she turned over several times between her delicate fingers.

'This is it,' Lara said, sounding relieved.

'Well, I'm glad we found it,' she replied, as she returned the worthless coins to the box.

'He told me about you and how you couldn't have babies.'

'That was very personal, considering he hardly knew you.'

'We met quite often. He was very kind to me, gave me a towel to dry my hair. A red towel,' she added, sadly.

'How long have you been meeting each other?'

'A few times last summer and a few times before he died. He told me how happy you were together.'

'How comforting. What is it you're looking for in life, apart from your coin?'

'A father figure, someone who will take care of me. An older man.'

'Not someone your own age?'

'Absolutely not, young men are unreliable.'

'Let's hope you can find one, unattached.'

'I believe you should follow your heart.'

'Whatever the cost to another?' she snapped. 'I take it you live around here.'

'In the village across the lake. I just come down in the summer.'

'You stay with friends or family?'

'Family,' Lara replied, shortly. 'I was thirteen when my mother died. I went to a foster home and left as quick as possible.'

'That is really sad. How old are you, dear?'

'Old enough to take care of myself,' Lara informed her sharply.

'I have an idea. We will put your bike in my boat and sail back to your village. That way I can show you where Lars died. Would you like that?'

'I know where Lars died. On Souls Island.'

'How do you know that?'

'Well, firstly, it was in all the local newspapers and, secondly, I found him. We were going to meet lunchtime, as before, but I found him dead. I didn't know what to do so I surfed back home.'

Kia stared, unfocused, into the garden and out over the grey water, her jaw clenched, her lips pulled into a thin tight line.

'That must have been a terrible shock for you. We did not find him until late afternoon. All those hours alone, waiting for us to come. Poor Lars', she whispered. 'He might have still been alive, how did you know for sure he was dead? Why didn't you get help, why didn't you go to the police?'

'I don't like the police.'

'Why not?'

'Because, that's why.'

'Tell you what,' Kia said, calmly, as though the incident was of little importance. 'I'll make a cup of my special tea and pick some flowers before we go. We can lay them on the beach. Would you like that?'

'Yes, I think that's a lovely idea. We can talk about Lars. Lars and Lara. Has a nice sound to it, don't you think?'

'If you say so,' she said, turning away in contempt. She walked slowly into the garden and gazed across at the Poppies and Daisies.

'Wild flowers in a wild garden,' she sighed, as she cut a brilliant red rose, pricking her finger as she did so. She sucked on the oozing blood and thought how a red rose, a symbol of love, could cause the giver or receiver pain. She wondered if love and blood were one, inevitably linked.

By the time she was halfway to the island, Lara was drifting in and out of sleep, her body relaxed while she gave little nods as her head fell forward. Eventually, she helped her to slump down into the bottom of the boat and quietly sailed to within a few meters of the island. She sat for a moment watching frills of bright green waterweed moving in time with the lapping water. She breathed deeply as she realised Lars would also have appreciated such beauty, such swaying rhyme.

She pulled herself together; this was not the time to be sentimental.

'Lara, get up. I think it's time you freshened up, perhaps a little dip might help,' she commanded.

The slender young girl swayed as she made the effort to stand but, before she could regain her balance, she fell clumsily over the side of the boat and into the cold water.

'You had better swim, dear, otherwise you might drown. We wouldn't want that now, would we?'

She watched Lara sputtering as she swallowed water, followed by a bout of heavy coughing as she splashed towards the beach.

'You left him. You left my Lars, my poor Lars. He was hours alone, waiting for me to find him. I would like to leave you here for hours. In fact, that is just what I am going to do. Here take your bike.' she shouted, hysterically, as she threw it and the bunch of flowers into the shallow water. She hesitated before throwing Lara's rucksack onto the beach since probably there was a much-needed mobile phone in it.

'You can cycle home, perhaps work a miracle; perhaps you might go down in the Guinness Book of Records. You can think yourself lucky I didn't tip you into the middle of the lake.'

Lara watched Kia manoeuver the sailboat further out into the lake as she tried to organise her dull mind. She was happy that Kia was so angry she might not remember much about the point of her visit, the coin. With a bit of luck her suggestive remarks about she and Lars might swamp all other emotions, though she had to admit she had rather overplayed her cards.

Anyway, she considered her mission to be a success as she pulled the bike out of the water and found her mobile phone in her rucksack. She stared at it for a few minutes while she tried to think up a good reason why she should be on an island with a bike.

'Now I really need to stretch my imagination, I hope you are feeling gullible today, dear sister,' she murmured, as she chose Freya's name.

*

'You took my bike without asking and now it's on an island. How the hell did you get that together?' Freya shouted, angrily, as she stepped out of a rowing boat onto the beach.

'Well it's so silly you probably won't believe me.'

'Try me.'

Lara took a deep breath. 'Well, it's like this. I cycled to the other side of the lake to meet a girlfriend but she did not turn up so I sat on a jetty for a while. Then, this old woman comes along in a sailboat. She asks me where I live and I pointed to our village. Then, she offered to take me home in her boat. Of course, I refused but she persisted and, in the end, I put your bike in the back of her boat.

She stops here, hands me a bunch of flowers and tells me to place them on a rock further down the beach. I was doing what she asked when I heard a splash. She had thrown your bike in the water and was sailing away. I salvaged your bike. That is why I am so wet. That was it,' she added, shrugging her shoulders.

'Unbelievable.'

'Told you, unbelievable.'

'Perhaps a little too unbelievable.'

'By the way, you know I found a coin last year, well it could be an old one.'

'No, I can't say I remember you telling me that.'

'I've been looking through some books on coins at the library,' Lara continued, ignoring Freya's lack of memory. 'It needs to be valued.'

'You know, Lara, you tell me the most ridiculous story of some old woman chucking you on the island with my bike of all things. Then you follow it up with a story of some coin, which you found a year ago, suddenly being valuable. Lara, how about the truth, just once tell the truth before the truth bites you in the butt.'

'It is the truth. An old woman did leave me on the island and I did read a book.'

'You are a fantasist, Lara, which is a polite way of saying you are a liar. In fact, I would go as far as to say you are a compulsive liar.'

'I know. I can't help it.'

'Get in the boat, you're rowing, and be careful with my bike. I want to get home, I have better things to do than run after you.'

The oars made ripples across the silent water as she yanked them through their holders. She loved the sound they made and lifted her face to catch the last sun of the day. It would soon be ice cold, too cold to windsurf, too cold to sleep in Freya's draughty loft. The tourists would have scuttled back to their warm homes, no longer finding the village interesting enough to battle the icy blasts sweeping across the lake.

She would return to a couple of rooms in the city where her stories would be of people who dealt in drugs and stolen goods; people wanted by the police; people who were desperate and did desperate things to survive.

She found it difficult to fantasise about the rich. She thought their problems were luxury problems unless, of course, she became one of them. It did not really matter, whichever way the coin fell, she lived in an exciting world. Her stories brought colour into her life and into the lives of her listeners who sometimes believed her or, more often than not, gave a half smile as they walked away.

Only Freya understood her, experienced life at its rawest. That was why the old coin was her only hope. If it was valuable then she and Freya could start a new life. Meanwhile, she would sleep in the attic and at the end of the summer return to a couple of rooms in the city supplied by the social services.

*

Kia sailed home aware of her dark thoughts for pushing Lara into the middle of the lake would have been easy. She had actually considered a murderous act and that had shocked her. She wondered whether others considered such a thing. She thought it probable though unlikely they would admit their dark side to themselves let alone to anyone else.

She closed her eyes and imagined Lars was sitting opposite her, laughing with her at the idea of Lara cycling across the lake with crowds of admirers waiting on the shoreline.

It seemed to Kia that evening, after the shock of Lara's indifference to her husband's death had lessened, that it was highly unlikely that Lars had dallied with a girl young enough to be his daughter or even his granddaughter. He might well have been flattered; even a little too charming, but she doubted it went much further than that since their lovemaking was little more than a few kisses and perhaps a caress or two. It seemed to her that neither she nor Lars had either the inclination or energy to relight the old flame. She had not thought that to be unusual.

Now, she was filled with doubt and tried to concentrate on how Lara had sat at the kitchen table, her fingers moving nimbly through the pile of loose change until her hand stopped and hovered over a piece of old metal. She had quickly picked it up, studied it on both sides, pushed it into the front pocket of her tight fitting jeans and secured it firmly with a zip. She had been too distressed to notice which coin she had taken though she could still hear the sound of the small zipper. She thought it strange how small things such as smells and sounds could be stored in the memory, filed away in the subconscious until needed. She also found it strange that Lara had not returned the coin to the locket still hanging around her neck. It was as if she had put it away, safely away, under lock and key.

She felt a need, an overwhelming need, to find this slip of a girl who had found it necessary to violate her memory of Lars. She would force her to show her the coin.

She decided a visit to the village just opposite the island was a good starting place, perhaps Lara Lindberg was known and easy to find and if not then she would visit the Library archives. For, surely, the local newspaper would have reported Lara's brave grandfather, perhaps even taken a photograph of him.

IT was an unusual little village with tiny shops huddled together supporting each other while their asymmetric roofs carelessly overlapped. Bric à brac, pottery, second hand books and handmade candles were for sale between local farming products and grocery stalls; an intriguing place where she felt very much at home.

Eventually, she stopped in front of a narrow shop selling spiritual objects; wind bells, Buddha's, pendants like the one she had, unusual stones and even angel and tarot cards. A sign in the window offered to buy antique objects and second hand jewellery and gold. Another smaller sign advertised the buying and selling of old coins.

'Coins,' she murmured. 'I wonder why that rings a bell. Lara, I think this little shop is worth a visit.'

A small bell tinkled as she entered attracting the attention of a young woman from behind a beaded curtain.

'Can I help you?' she asked, hopefully.

'Yes, I'm looking for a keepsake for a little boy.'

'Have you anything in mind,' asked the rather hippy young woman who had rows of coloured beads hanging around her neck.

'I thought perhaps a coin.'

'We have a nice collection of Ducats. They are not too expensive. She pulled out a drawer of neatly placed coins.

'Oh, they are lovely. Coins last forever.'

'Not diamonds?' the girl laughed.

'Yes, but I am too poor to buy diamonds. A coin will have to do,' she smiled, joining in the joke. 'I once met a very nice young woman. She said she lived around here. She was also interested in coins.'

'Do you know her name?'

'Lara Lindberg, I believe.'

'Oh, Lara, she's my sister. She comes here to help, mostly this time of year. I think she sees it as a holiday.'

'Well, you can't blame her. Is she here now?'

'No, she went back to town early this morning.'

'When is she coming back?'

'No idea. She drops in when she feels like it. Where did you meet Lara?' she girl added, sounding slightly worried.

'On the beach. She had been windsurfing and I asked her if the water was not too cold. We struck up a conversation about wetsuits.'

'That's Lara alright. A water baby if ever there was one.'

'Well, some babies are born in a tub of water.'

The young woman smiled, sweetly, as she handed her a small neatly wrapped box tied with a blue ribbon. 'That's true, but I happen to know she was born in a hospital bed. I hope you will come again,' she added.

'I will be back if only to snoop around the shelves.'

'You never know what you might find,' the girl laughed, loudly. 'Who shall I say called?'

'Mrs. Nielson, Kia Nielson.'

*

Freya Lindberg watched Kia Nielson leave her shop and walk slowly down to the moorings adjoining the beach. She had not been suspicious when the rather homely woman first wandered around her shop but now a feeling of apprehension ran through her for she had shown an interest in Lara. She hoped Kia's visit was pure coincidence but she did not believe in coincidences and her instinct told her that Kia's visit was not without reason. She thought coins were the common denominator since Lara had followed up her story of the old woman with another about a coin. It was more than likely Kia Nielson had become aware of the past and that posed a threat to her vulnerable sister.

She chose a name in her mobile. Lara answered.

'You know who has been here, asking after you?'

'No, who?'

'Kia Nielson, I guess she was the woman who threw my bike into the lake and left you on the island. Why would she do that?'

'Listen, I have to go. I am dropping in at my flat. I'll be back this evening.'

'Don't stall, Lara. We have to talk.'

'I know.'

'I hope to God you haven't done anything stupid. I've told you so often, don't draw attention to yourself.'

'I am attractive, so I attract people.'

'Shut up, I don't want to hear your rubbish.'

Lara was careful not to wake Freya as she carefully climbed the narrow stairs to the attic that night. Her visit to the auction house had been unsuccessful since they were renovating and various coin dealers closed for the holidays. She would have to wait a little longer to have the coin valued and that irritated her. She puffed on one of her 'joints' to compensate for her wasted day and hoped the unusual smell of Cannabis would be gone before Freya woke up in the morning, though her habit was no secret.

She watched the smoke rise slowly towards a small window in the roof as she recalled how years before she had sat on the narrow wooden stairs at the back of Freya's shop. A man had taken her sister's hand in his and tenderly stroked it.

Eventually, he left but not before he held Freya tightly in his arms, giving her a little reassuring shake while she stood with her head bowed, thanking him profusely.

'I have to take you back,' Freya had said, after closing the door behind the man.

'Who was that?'

'A nice man who helps people like me. He owns this place and I don't have to pay any rent until I get a business started. If I ever get one started,' she added.

'What does he want in return?'

'Nothing, as far as I know.'

'And if he does?'

'I'll think about it when the time comes. Come on, put on your coat. We have to go.'

'Must we?'

'It's only for a little while longer then you can live with me.'

'My social worker is trying to find me a couple of rooms in the city centre when I leave those people.'

'Do you want that?'

'Here in the summer, town centre in the winter. I can't get it better than that, can it?'

'Whatever you want,' Freya had replied, wearily.

Lara continued to place shreds of Cannabis carefully over cheap tobacco and rolled another 'joint' as she turned her thoughts back again to when she had been wind surfing about two years ago. Her sail had needed checking and she had jumped into shallow water near to a small island, unaware that the occupant of a small sailboat was fishing.

She had immediately recognised the man who had held her sister in his arms. Freya would not discuss him and insisted their friendship was platonic. She had argued that platonic did not exist.

'Sorry, I've disturbed the fish,' she had cooed.

'They are not biting, probably the wrong time of day.'

He bent over to the back of the boat and offered her a towel. 'Here, dry yourself off,' he said.

She had noted how he was dressed in light coloured trousers, sandals and a checked shirt. His once blond hair had greyed. She thought he was an attractive man and had probably been so all his life. She could imagine women falling for him.

'Want one?' he asked, as he poured a cup of coffee from an old thermos flask.

They had sat chatting for a while and she had told him how she had stayed in a foster home after her parents died and how she had left as quickly as possible. She had hoped that a few personal details of her life might encourage him to mention his. Perhaps why he knew Freya well enough to hold her in his arms.

He had sympathised. 'I would have taken you in. My wife was unable to have children.'

'Sorry to hear that. Perhaps you saved yourselves a lot of trouble.'

'Perhaps.'

'Life's a bitch.'

'What makes you say that?' he asked, kindly.

'I am broke, have no job and I do not want one. That makes me a loser.'

'I don't think you are a loser. You are very beautiful. You should use your assets.'

'How?'

'You must be very photogenic. I know a photographer. He is always looking for new models.'

'Really, do you think he would photograph me?'

'I am sure he would.'

'Do I get into magazines?'

'If you are lucky. Who knows? What did you say your name was?'

'Lara and yours?'

'Lars,' he replied, evasively, as though embarrassed.

'Lars and Lara, has a nice sound to it, don't you think?' she giggled, still hoping he might offer a few details of his life. 'That photographer,' she added, as though it was not important, 'Where can I find him?'

That was how she met Connor, Irish father, American mother.

She knew it was her choice, she knew he was sleazy, she could see that quite quickly, but she did not care. She was seventeen and in love with Connor.

She only wanted him to love her, admire her. She would do anything he asked. She was his, body and soul. She was his.

She allowed her blurred thoughts to run like a film through her mind, her memories of Connor's kisses, his caresses until she could no longer contain her screams. He had taken photographs of her in all positions. She had not minded; she had done it to please him; to make him want her. There was no end to his demands. Then, suddenly, it was over. He was too busy to see her that week, he would pick her up at the weekend, but he never came. She had watched him one evening leaving his studio with a girl perhaps even younger than she was. She had watched them get into his car; watched as he moved his hand across the girl's long bare legs before he pulled the seatbelt over her breasts. She had cried all the way home to Freya.

It was nearly a year later before she met Lars again. He was fishing as before in his boat off the island. She was not particularly happy to meet him but she decided she owed him a dose of her imagination after he had introduced her to Connor Finley.

She wondered whether he knew about Connor's special bedroom above his studio and his preferences. She even wondered if Lars had handed her over to him, perhaps he had done that before. Found vulnerable young girls and passed them over to Connor.

Lars had greeted her enthusiastically and asked whether she had appeared on the front cover of a magazine. She had told him how Connor had taken a series of photographs and would let her know if he could sell them to the media.

He seemed to accept her story and carried on talking about everyday affairs. In fact, she had found him rather boring and thought it was time for a little storytelling, just to liven things up. Then, she would drop a hint or two about Freya to see if he reacted.

'I got busted for possession,' she informed him, waiting for the usual reaction.

'Cannabis?'

'Yep. Now I've a police record.'

'Naughty girl. Keep off the rubbish.'

'I am off.'

'Why did you go on?'

'Connor. Because of Connor,' she half lied.

'Connor?' he queried.

'The photographer who likes porno.'

'He took advantage of you?'

'Are you surprised?'

'I didn't know. I'll have a talk with him.'

'Don't bother. He's dead meat.'

'I'll see he doesn't do that again.'

'How?'

'I have a way,' he muttered.

'My grandfather was given a coin for bravery,' she said, totally changing the subject.

'Really, that is something. Your family must have been very proud of him.'

'And my father collected old coins. He knew a lot about them.'

'I also collected coins but they were valueless. At least, I paid too much for them. Amateur enthusiasm, I have just one left over, keep meaning to bring it to an expert.' he stared ahead as though remembering something. 'Found it in a box at a car boot sale, in England. I have no idea if it is old or not. It is probably nothing. I'll show it to you, one day.'

'I would love to see it. I will be here the day after tomorrow, same time. You could bring it with you.'

'I'll have to find it. It's probably between piles of loose change left over from trips abroad.'

'Where do you live?' she asked.

'In a log house between the trees, over there,' he replied, pointing to a cluster of trees on the other side of the lake. 'I used to work in the timber trade. And, where do you live?'

'In the village, over there.' She stood up as she pointed across the lake. 'My sister has a little shop selling antique jewellery and stuff like that.'

'Can she make a living?'

'Well, only if she gets financial help from an admirer,' she teased. 'You must come and visit us. We live on the quay. Lovely in the summer but I hate the winter. Do you ever go there? It is full of tourists this time of year. Freya is quite busy that is why I must go.'

'Take care,' he answered, thoughtfully.

'I'll be okay.'

'I'll keep an eye on you, just in case.'

'Don't forget to come, day after tomorrow, same time, same place,' she shouted, as she climbed on her surfboard and turned the sail to catch the wind.

He had kept his promise, she could see his sailboat bobbing in the water, he waved and she waved back.

'Where's the coffee?' she shouted.

He helped her to climb up into the boat and, as before, handed her the soiled towel. She thought he was fatherly towards her, concerned. She liked that, made her feel wanted, a luxury lacking in her difficult life, only she was unsure whether he was about to introduce her to yet another sleazy acquaintance. She thought that would be exciting only next time she would be ready.

'So,' she asked after having drunk the coffee, 'Where is it? Where's your old coin?'

He looked startled. 'Oh, I forgot it. I am sorry. My wife was a bit angry at my going off again. I will bring it tomorrow. I looked it up on the Internet. I think I've got something rather special.'

'What then?'

'It could date back to the seventeenth century.'

'Really!'

'Only said could. I must have it valued. Should have done that years ago, never thought much about it.'

She had been angry and shouted at him for not remembering to bring it. She had looked forward to seeing it and now she had to wait another day.

She noticed how he suddenly looked tired and she apologised for being so bad tempered. It was only because she was disappointed. It was only because she would like to see it for herself.

He had looked away as though hurt by her verbal attack. 'I am sorry,' he apologised again.

She looked into his grey eyes. They were sad, almost pleading as though looking for kindness. She stood up and sat next to him, stroking his grey hair and running the back of her hand down his cheek as a mother would a child.

'Tomorrow is another day. It doesn't matter,' she said, softly as she slipped her wet suit down to her waist and pulled a T-shirt off her body.

He said nothing as she sat astride his lap and gently rocked 'to and fro'. He said nothing as she kissed him and placed his hand on her breast.

She smiled at the idea that he had held Freya in his arms, now she held him. She wondered what Freya would think and feel if she ever found out. For just a moment, she felt power over Freya.

Suddenly, he slumped forward. She could see his face was wet with perspiration. He lifted his head and she thought he wanted to say something but instead he gave a heave as though the last air was leaving his lungs. He remained motionless except for a few last gasps.

She had waited for a moment, shocked that she had seen yet another person die in her short life. She had been young when, early one morning, she witnessed a dreadful scene. She had gone back to bed and hidden under the duvet pretending it had not happened. She had never told anyone that she had shared her mother's last moments of life. It was her secret. Her mother's last moments on earth were hers.

She looked around the lake but there was no one in sight. Just she and a dead man.

She had lowered her head in respect and said how sorry she was before she slid over the side of the boat and surfed back home as though nothing had happened. The cool wind blew in her face as she considered how she might be able to obtain a coin that was not hers. A coin that just might be of value. In any case, meeting Lars' wife would give her information that she could add to her book about people. People she knew well and even those she did not know well. She had once read that information was power.

Of course, she could not do anything until after the funeral. She had decided the best way of attack would be 'shock and awe', before the grieving widow had time to collect her thoughts.

Freya had come from behind the beaded curtain as she entered the shop.

'Get dressed', she had said angrily. 'You have to go shopping. It's almost closing time'.

'I'll buy a cake to celebrate.'

'Celebrate what?'

'The future.'

'Future? You have no future unless you stop puffing. Do something useful for a change. Get a life.'

A few days later, she read in the local newspaper that Lars Nielson, a well-known philanthropist in the area, had died of a heart attack while fishing off Souls Island. It went on to say how he supported young people beginning new projects and businesses and that he will be missed by the local community.

'So, Lars,' she had murmured. 'I think your wife deserves a visit. I need to get hold of your coin.'

It did not surprise Kia when Axel Hansson telephoned. She knew he would do so, give or take a few weeks, after all settling a testament was a long procedure. What did surprise her was the reason why he phoned.

'Do you remember I told you Lars ended a lease on a photograph shop?'

'Yes,' she replied, carefully.

'Well, I have had the tenant on the phone. He heard how Lars had died just after he had cancelled his lease. He was wondering if you would lengthen it for just a little longer. It seems his business is just beginning to show a profit and moving at this time would not help. He would like to contact you, if you have no objections.'

'No,' she replied, 'anything to help a beginner. What is his name?'

'Connor Finley'.

'Fine, I'll let you know what I decide.'

Connor telephoned her almost immediately after her call with Axel. He sounded a nice young man, polite and enthusiastic as he explained how his Studio had finally become viable.

He was a successful wedding photographer and had even sold pictures to magazines. He needed just a little more time to find another place near to where he was now. His lease terminated in December and he hoped she might lengthen it.

'Would you like to visit my Studio then you can see for yourself how I've set it up and how important it is for me to get established for just a little longer.'

'I might be going away for a few days.'

'You can come whenever you like. The shop is closed on Mondays, gives me a bit of time to balance the books,' he added, sounding embarrassed. 'Can you manage that?'

She liked Connor, his friendly smile, thick dark hair and sparkling brown eyes. She knew she would lengthen the lease on his studio if only because he was attractive.

'So, tell me how you arrived in Sweden. Connor Finley is obviously an English name.'

'Actually, my father was Irish. My American mother met my Swedish stepfather when I was eight years old and we came here to live. I still hold an Irish passport.'

'That is an interesting mix. Now, what about your lease.'

'The business is beginning to take off. Of course, I do the normal things, passport photo's, weddings, etc., but I have made a few good contacts in the media world. Also internationally. Sometimes I go abroad to photograph wild life. I have even sold photographs of models to magazines. Swedish girls are special. Or perhaps I'm a little bias,' he laughed.

She glanced at the glossy photographs hanging on the walls of naturally beautiful young women.

'I have many more,' he added, taking several books from out of a cupboard. 'These are the ones who did not make it, so to speak. All lovely girls but it is almost impossible for them to get started.'

She took a book out of politeness and flipped through the pages. They all looked the same to her, mostly blond beauties with a dark haired one in between. She really was not interested. Perhaps she even felt a little irritated at their aspirations; to be admired for their beauty. She wondered if she was jealous or just too down to earth for such a purposeless goal in life.

She was just about to hand the book back to Connor when a photograph of a young girl caught her attention. She held the book to the light.

'I think I know her. Isn't that Lara Lindberg?'

Connor took the book from her. 'Yes, it is.'

'I met her and her sister, Freya. Small world. Didn't know she was interested in modelling.'

'I am afraid she was one of the unlucky ones. I sent her photographs around but, as I said, the chance of being noticed is very small.'

'Did she tell you she is interested in old coins?'

'No, not that I can remember.'

'She told me a story of how her grandfather saved the crew of a fishing boat and the local town people gave him an old coin for his bravery.'

Connor chuckled loudly, a deep Irish chuckle.

'Typical Lara story, never met anyone like her. Actually, we went out for a few weeks but I broke it off when her stories became too bizarre. I found her rather sad.'

'Is it true that the girls lost both parents?'

'Yes, I believe so.'

'How long ago was it?'

'Around five years. Lara went into Care but her sister not, she was just that bit older.'

'Poor girls.'

'Freya told me how some sympathetic benefactor, we both know who that was, set her up with the shop. Don't tell them I told you.'

She frowned as she tried to understand his remark about a benefactor. 'No, of course not. No wonder Lara lives in a dream world.'

'And the lease?'

'I will tell my solicitor to renew it on a yearly basis.'

'What about Freya?'

'What about her?'

'Her lease. Will you be lengthening that as well?'

She drew her breath in as she tried to absorb what he said. 'I will have to ask Freya what she would like. If she wants me to extend the lease, then I will. After all, the girls have had enough unhappiness in their lives without my adding to it.'

'That will make her happy. Come any time you want, passport photos or any other photo for that matter.'

She stayed a little longer talking about his various visits to Ireland. He had even met a boy who remembered him from the junior school.

She sat in her car for a few minutes aware she had visited Freya's shop without knowing it had belonged to Lars. Benefactor, what did that entail? Did Freya know who she was when she was in her shop? Probably not until she gave her name. So why didn't she say something?

'I want to visit dear Axel again. I need to see that list of rentals. I need to know who is on it.'

*

Axel handed her the list. 'You didn't have to come, I would have sent it to you,' he said, fondly. 'It's good you take an interest. Something to keep you busy.'

'Strange,' she replied. 'My having a portfolio. I feel quite the property owner and I want to carefully consider what to do next. I wish I had taken more interest in what Lars did. He told me he renovated houses with his friends. As far as I know, he saw it as a sort of hobby.'

'That's right, a couple of retired builders, old friends, did the work. He liked getting his hands dirty but not too often,' he laughed. 'He was a bit of a philanthropist, helped young people in trouble to get started. He was a very modest man, never spoke about what he did.'

'Well, he didn't like getting his hands dirty in the garden either.'

Alex laughed. 'He's not the only one. The Will is simple. Just leave everything to me,' he continued.

'In your very capable hands. Oh, by the way,' she added, running her finger down the list of properties. 'I believe he rented a shop to a Freya Lindberg. I can't see it here'.

'Yes, he did but he sold it.'

'Okay,' she answered, relieved that she did not have to make a decision regarding the tenancy.

He shook her hand warmly. 'Lars was a good man,' he repeated.

'You know what they say?' she said.

'No, tell me.'

'No good deed goes unpunished,' she replied, almost seriously.

'I am afraid that is true,' replied Axel, thoughtfully.

Freya felt successful. She had managed to buy some nice antiques including a porcelain doll at a good price. She was brushing her hair when Kia Nielson entered her shop.

'How can I help you, Mrs. Nielson?' she asked, sounding anxious.

'You remember my name, I'm impressed.'

'Of course. What do you think of her?' she asked, smoothing the doll's hair. 'I have just bought her in a clear-out sale.'

'She is lovely.'

'Are you here to buy or just looking around?'

'Neither, I am looking for Lara.'

'Because?'

'The coin she found is most probably mine. She came to my house after my husband's funeral. She spun me a story that she had given a coin to Lars and he would check to see if it was of any value. She took it before I had a chance to see it. I remembered, after she had left, that Lars also had an old coin and now I want to see the one she took.'

'Are you suggesting she stole it?'

'No, she did not steal it. In fact, I am not sure what she did. If anything, she conned me.'

'She has not told me anything about it,' replied Freya, untruthfully.

'She also said she was with Lars when he died.'

'Not again, surly not,' Freya whispered.

'What do you mean by not again?'

'My father drove out of the drive and a car crashed into the side of it, on my mother's side. She died almost instantly. Lara heard the crash and ran to the car. My father died six months later of a stroke and, once again, Lara was in the house alone with him. It was after that she started to fantasise.'

'Poor girl. You know the coin is not that important,' she said, realising how trivial it all was, compared to the misery the girls had suffered. 'Anyway, I would like to see Lara again. Do you know where I can find her?'

'She will be here tomorrow but I don't think she is that keen on meeting you.'

'I can understand that. One of her stories was a bit over the top.'

'Which one of her many stories would that be?'

'It was not what she said but what she implied. We'll leave it at that.'

'She can't help it. I'm sorry if she upset you.'

'Already forgotten. Tell Lara to come and see me. Tell her I am truly sorry she was present when my husband died. Perhaps she will let me see the coin,' she laughed, lightly.

She left the shop none the wiser regarding Connor's off-hand remark about a benefactor. It did not matter, she would slowly work her way into Freya's world.

*

Kia watched Lara cycling against the wind towards her house. It was some way to cycle across the bridge and along the roads running parallel with the lake. Her face was flush and her hair wild when she eventually sat down in her kitchen.

'Good that you could make it. It's a long way to come,' she said, warmly.

Lara did not reply.

'Would you like a drink, perhaps a coca cola instead of tea?' she suggested.

'Fine.'

'So, tell me what have you been doing?' she asked, her hand shook as she poured the cola into a glass. Lara made her nervous and she felt angry that she had such an effect on her.

'Nothing.'

'There must be something that interests you. Even if only a hobby.'

'There is a Silversmith and Jewellery Course starting soon. I would love to do that and Freya could help sell my things in her shop.' She paused. 'But I don't have the money. That is why the coin is so important.'

'Forget the coin. I think that is a lovely idea. I can see you doing something like that. So, when does the Course begin?'

'September.'

'Well, then, write yourself in. See it as a gift for all the stress you must have had when my husband died.'

Lara sat motionless as though her world had stopped.

'Would you pay for the Course, would you really do that?'

'Yes, Lara, I would like to do that,' she answered, kindly.

'Thank you,' she squealed. 'I have to tell Freya. Thank you.'

Kia felt unusually tired after Lara left. Somehow, the young woman sucked her energy and she was angry with herself that she had not mentioned the coin. After all, that was the reason for her visit. Now she was unsure whether her offer for the Course was such a good idea. After all, it was possible that Lara's nimble fingers might pocket any silver carelessly left around.

She feared she might have courted disaster by being involved with a couple of dubious young women.

*

She was in the kitchen when Lara arrived, unexpectedly, over a week later.

'I thought we might have a picnic on Souls Island.'

'What a surprise,' she answered.

'I love surprises.'

'Just give me a minute.'

'No hurry,' Lara replied as she sat on a garden chair with her face lifted to the weak sun.

'Did you tell Freya about the Silversmith Course?' she asked as she closed the windows and locked the door.

'Yes'

'And?'

'She said you should stay out of our business.'

'Well, that's a 'thank you'. I shall stay out of your business when I know it is not my business.'

'What is that supposed to mean?'

'Nothing. I want to talk to Freya.'

'I am going home.'

'That's fine by me. What changed? You want to go on a picnic and then you don't. I can't follow you.'

'You don't have to follow me. I have just changed my mind. That's all.'

'Nobody just changes their mind without a reason.'

'Freya has just messaged to say she does not want you talking to me, interfering in our affairs. She says we have enough money for my Course. Anyway, she is not going to tell you anything. I have been trying for years to find out what the man wanted.'

'Who are you talking about?'

'Your husband, who else.'

She felt her mouth become dry from anxiety. 'Perhaps he did not want anything. Perhaps he was just kind.'

'Come on, nothing is for nothing. Lars introduced me to Connor, the porno photographer. How is that for kind?'

A headache formed behind her eyes. 'I will come behind it. Whatever, the truth is, I will find out.'

'Leave it alone,' warned Lara. 'Sometimes it is better not to know the truth. Sometimes it is better to stay ignorant.'

'How wise you suddenly are since the word 'truth' is not even in your vocabulary.'

She hardly turned her head when Lara picked up her bike and cycled quickly away.

What should have been a nice afternoon had turned out to be just another disaster to add to all the other bloody disasters in her life. She had lost faith in all she believed in; all she had taken for granted; one big myth; one big lie. She looked out at the garden and the red roses Lars had planted and she had tended. Their dying petals laid upon the earth as pools of velvet red blood.

'I am stuck,' she thought. 'I am in Limbo.'

She could see Freya smoking a cigarette behind the beaded curtains. She made no effort to greet her although the doorbell tinkled as she entered. It was obvious Freya wanted to make a statement.

'I have been expecting you,' she said, coolly. 'I hear you have been talking to Lara.'

'I want a few honest answers.'

'Depends on the questions.'

'Did you have something with my husband?'

'Of course not,' Freya scorned. 'Why do you think Lara has that name?'

'What must I guess?'

Lars is, or rather was, Lara's father. She does not know and I have no reason to tell her. I am happy with it as it is. We don't need more and we don't need you.'

She grasped the counter as the room swung around her.

'Lars had an affair with my mother around twenty years ago. She worked in an estate agent's office. She told me a week before she died that she was planning to tell my father about Lars.'

'Why, why did she want to tell your father after so long?'

'Because she thought Lars should contribute to keeping his child. He was rich, my father had lost his job and my mother was struggling to keep things together. She needed money. She died before telling my father. Just as well.'

'And you did not tell Lara about her real father.'

'No.'

'How do you know Lars is Lara's father?'

'My mother kept his DNA, for a rainy day so to speak. She showed me the DNA report. I have it upstairs if you want to see it. Money, money, money,' she sneered. 'My father was not perfect but he did not deserve to hear her truth for the sake of money. Not after so many years. He loved Lara as his own child for thirteen years. I told my mother to put up and shut up.'

Kia sighed as she sat down. 'So Lara did not know Lars was her father when she met him on the island.'

'No, though she saw him when he came here but he did not see her'

'Why did he come here?' she asked, shortly.

'Lars had already bought this shop for his charity work,' Freya gave a grunt of disapproval. 'Charity begins at home,' she almost spat the words out. 'My mother told him that he was Lara's father when she was born. He said he did not want to have any trouble with my father so he ignored it. He said he would think about it. He never did.

After my parents died, he let me have this shop. One of his good deeds for the day. The afternoon Lara saw him here was the afternoon he told me how he wanted to do the right thing. He would transfer the Deeds of the shop into our joint names. I would be trustee for Lara until she was of age. He said it was better not to tell her he was her father since she was innocent of the whole affair. He said he would change his testament to include her. As you know, he never did. Probably a step too far,' she added bitterly.

'No, she was not in his Will but still he gave you the shop.

He must have had a guilty conscience. What a mess,' Kia whispered. 'I knew nothing about it. If he had only told me, we could have taken care of Lara after your parents died. It was his child and he left her. How could he do that? He should have owned up. Told me the truth. He turned his back on his own child,' she murmured.

'Perhaps he did not believe Lara was his child, perhaps he thought my mother was lying.'

'If he had really wanted to know he could have asked for the DNA results. He took the easy way out and I suspect your mother had no option than to keep quiet and hope your father would never find out. So typical.'

'Yes, you are right. If she had told him, he would have divorced her. They were not happy together.'

'Perhaps Lars loved me and didn't want to hurt me,' she added, sadly.

'You know what I think might have happened.'

'What?'

'Well, Lara meets him on the island, tells him where she lives, talks about me and, of course, he realises she is his daughter. Perhaps meeting her face to face was too much. Perhaps it caused him to have a heart attack.'

'What shall I do now?' she sighed.

'Do what is right.'

'And that is?'

'Recognise Lara as your late husband's child.'

'I don't particularly like her,' she admitted.

'Try to be patient,' Freya replied, hopefully.

'She said Lars offered her a red towel to dry herself. We never had a red towel. What is that about?'

'She took a towel and tried to stop the bleeding on my mother's face. They found her in bed clutching it. Her hands covered in blood. Then, just six months later, my father died of a Stroke. Perhaps caused by the accident. Anyway, she did not speak for ages. I even thought she would never talk again. When she did, it was as now, one big fantasy. Maybe it will stop one day.'

Kia stood up and walked quickly to the door.

'I have to talk to Axel. He has to end a lease and so much more,' she added as she rushed out of the shop.

Her visit to Axel was short and tense when she informed him to end Connor Finley's lease and, furthermore, she wished to change her last Will and Testament.

Axel had asked if she had carefully considered her decision; was she not still too emotional after her husband's death.

She had stood in front of his desk, shaking in anger. 'You lied to me. You knew damned well that Lars secretly gave away the shop to those girls. You also know why he gave it to them. I can think of no one who deserves my estate more than Freya Lindberg and Lara Nielson-Lindberg, who is Lars' child, as you well know.

That is what I want. Please put it in order as soon as possible. Yesterday will be fine.'

He had looked stunned when she had left his office. Perhaps he did not know about Lara but she thought he did.

Kia chose a windy day to sail one last time to the island before winter set in. She wanted to stand and scream in the wind at Lars. Scream at what she knew he had done. Scream at what she did not know he had done. She would scream at how much she hated him, despised him, scream at how much she had loved him, unconditionally loved him, only for him to cheat on her.

Only after she had signed her Last Will and Testament did she cry. Only after she had settled what Lars morally owed.

The island was deserted and dark clouds were lying thick and low when she moored in the grey choppy water. She shivered as she jumped into the shallows and waded to the stony beach where she threw a plastic bin bag onto the thinly grassed ground, sat down and stared at the small white heads of waves beaten up by the wind.

It occurred to her that the last months of uncertainty would not have happened if Lara had not come to her house with a ridiculous story about a coin. Axel would have covered up the gift of the shop to Freya and Lara. She would never have found out about Lars' love child and Lara's stupid greed and fantasising would have stayed on the other side of the lake.

A flash of lightning zig zagged through the dark sky and large drops of rain began to fall slowly followed by slanting sleet.

One tree, one old oak tree, ruled over the island. This was why the island was a favourite picnic ground, where the children climbed between the dry branches and even into its hollow middle. Little girls believed fairies lived there and a fairy ring further in the wooded area supported their fantasy.

'Oh, Lars,' she whispered. 'You had a child. You made a little girl and you did not tell me.'

She realised she was not shouting as she had planned but crying, her tears undiscernible from the rain. She almost wanted to laugh. Here she was, stranded by the storm on the island where Lars had died and where she had left Lara with Freya's bike. Poetic justice, she thought.

She began to count between the thunder and the flashes; aware there was no time between them. When she looked up Lars was sitting in the moored boat. The float at the end of his fishing line bobbed up and down in the choppy water. He waved.

'Come and join me,' he called.

She heard a noise, perhaps a cracking noise, and felt green leaves sweeping her face as branches fell heavily upon her body; precursor to the final blow from the massive ancient trunk.

She thought she must atone for her sins but, surely, God asked for sacrifice not suffering. Surely, God must now be satisfied.

*

Emilie Nielson stood above her crushed body aware she had no place in the physical world, no human feelings.

She was in a place of light without shadows. A place where searching for happiness was unnecessary for she was in happiness.

Her spirit called the ones she loved and together they would dream understanding they were within a dimension of transcendent thought.

She called Lars. They would meet without words, only a knowing of each other and of all things.

Without judgement.

Lara Lindberg was for the first time alone in Kia's house. Now her house; now Freya's house. She found Lars' box of worthless coins and spread them over the table aware she was repeating history, aware she was not alone. She ignored any lurking fears. She did not believe in ghosts or hauntings, she was very sober about those things.

She had taken the coin to a Dealer who said it was worth a great deal of money. He had auctioned it and paid several thousand into her own bank account. She had insisted on that, her own bank account, and Freya had reluctantly agreed. She did not think she needed to share the money from the sale of the coin, not now Freya had inherited half of Kia's estate, which did not make her happy. She did not see why Freya should benefit. Lars was not her father. He had nothing to do with her unless, of course, there was more to their friendship than Freya was willing to tell.

She left the house and sat on the jetty watching the lights of the village flickering across the other side of the lake. Probably one of them was Freya's shop. She had planned to return home but dark clouds were forming and she felt too tired to cycle so far. She suddenly had an idea. She could sleep on Kia's couch, she had noticed a neatly folded blanket and she thought that was enough to keep her warm.

She messaged Freya to say that she would stay the night at Kia's house. It was going to rain and she had not brought a jacket. Freya messaged back telling her to lock the doors and windows at night.

Lara returned the mobile phone to her rucksack and took out her wallet, something she did often since she enjoyed looking at her new driving licence. She gazed admiringly at her photograph and thought she could sweet talk any police officer who stopped her for speeding. Only her name irritated her since it had to be the same name as on her birth certificate. She hated her grandmother's name but, luckily, her mother had given her a second name. One she always used. Of course, her mother had a good reason for choosing her second name, Lara.

She had been shocked when she found out Lars Nielson was her father. She guessed she was responsible for his death, her father's death. Her sexual game was probably too much for him since he must have known she was his daughter. She brushed it aside. It was his own fault. He did it himself. He should have known better than to mess with her. No harm done.

She giggled. Emiline Lara Lindberg was, actually, Emiline Lara Nielson.

She rubbed the locket hanging around her neck with her thumb. She had no idea of the consequences when she spun the story to Kia on that summer's afternoon. How could she have known Kia was her stepmother or Lars her father. She found that incredibly strange. In fact, almost beyond belief.

Poor Kia, she thought fondly. You did the right thing settling our finances for life. I guess it was your time to die. She frowned at the thought of them both dying on Souls Island.

However, there was a problem. Freya was becoming rather enamoured with a new boyfriend. One that might well marry her and share the half of Freya's inheritance. 'Good money down the drain,' she thought.

Everything would return to normal with the boyfriend out of the way. She decided he was expendable. It would take some time for Freya to recover from his demise but that was of little importance. She would wait for the right time, preferably in the very near future. Any death must look like an accident. It would take a good deal of planning but she did not see any serious problem though time was not on her side.

She also considered her future with Freya. Perhaps after a year or two, she would also become expendable. After all, another beau was bound to turn up. 'Money down the drain again. I don't think so,' she whispered.

She puffed on another 'joint' and decided to stay the winter with Freya.

The log house was cold. She would not be there if Freya's new boyfriend had helped her to buy a car when she wanted. That irritated her. She hated to wait for other people to do something. That was another good reason to support her rather radical decision about his future.

She looked around for a heater but she was unable to find one and it seemed that the wood burner was the only possibility. She swore under her breath when she carried armfuls of wood from outside into the house.

It really was not her scene, lighting fires and getting her hands dirty scraping out the cinders and ash from some previous fire, probably laid by Kia. That gave her another weird feeling and she questioned if staying the night on the couch was such a good idea.

The fire was crackling when Lara balanced a cup of soup on her lap with a couple of pieces of bread she had found in the freezer. It was not much but a bar of chocolate along with a mug of instant coffee would probably take her until the next day.

She threw a tartan blanket over herself and fell asleep but not before finding a bottle of rather good red wine.

It seemed Lara had drunk a large quantity of wine that night and had fallen into a deep sleep. The authorities reported that the previous owner had not swept the chimney for some considerable years. It had caught fire during the night and spread across the roof and down into the house.

They found Lara lying in the bathroom with a key in her hand but she was probably unable to focus on placing it in the lock. The windows were also shuttered and difficult to open. She had died of smoke inhalation.

Freya moved away from the area but first she arranged for the planting of a new Oak tree where the last one had stood for nearly one hundred years.

A brass plate read:

'In memory of Lars and Kia Nielson
Sleep Softly
on
Souls Island.'

She also placed a park bench overlooking the lake and village where she and Lara had lived.

Another brass plate read:

'In loving memory of Emeline Lara Lindberg-Nielson
Sadly missed'

After all, Freya could never have guessed Lara's plans for her future and how close she might have come to her death.

As Lara once said, 'Sometimes it is better not to know the truth. Sometimes it is better to stay ignorant.'

# AN INSIGNIFICANT LOVE AFFAIR

Felicity watched the gardener empty the bin of newly mown grass onto the compost heap, its sweet smell drifted across the lawn to where she laid on the hammock. She closed her eyes trying to recollect how Guy looked, how his hair fell in a lock over his forehead, the curls at the nape of his neck and his aftershave lotion that she found almost intoxicating. Her body became alive at his nearness but always she remained distant, indifferent, fearing rejection, fearing his ardour would cool once she submitted. She would never let that happen, she would never let herself succumb to the pain of lost love.

Eventually, Guy had drifted away and she had watched her girlfriend, Louisa, replace her. She could still remember her bitterness when they married, how she had walked numbly between their mutual friends at the reception and toasted to their happy life together.

She knew she had too much to drink when Guy cornered her, pushed her behind a pillar and kissed her bare neck and shoulders. He gently released her breasts from within her dress and caressed them while he ran his hand over her body. She could feel the heat within her and the wanting that had never been satisfied.

'Come,' he had whispered. 'I want to remember you for the rest of my life, I want to remember you.'

They had slipped away, unnoticed, into an empty bedroom. She wondered why she had held back for all those months. How now she found it permissible when before she had not.

She realised how a mistress had so little to lose and a wife so much. She thought she had lost but now she had won. For a short moment in time, a short moment of passion, she had won. Louisa had lost.

*

A year later, she and Harry Harriman had a whirlwind marriage, alone in a registry office. No frills or partying. Just a ceremony of promises and then to a hotel and bed. It had been romantic without romance. His love was passionate but she could not return the excruciating pain of satisfaction. Later, she learned to fake her heights. She thought he was too busy with himself to notice anything was wrong. She did not even want him to guess anything was wrong, she did not even want to reach the height she had on Louisa's wedding day. She was a cheat without cheating.

Then it happened. Two weeks ago, she had received a phone call from Louisa. She really did not want to meet her. She did not want to see the satisfaction of her life with Guy. Louisa insisted.

She had arranged to meet her in a small restaurant off 'Piccadilly'. She sat in an alcove and the waiter had automatically handed her the Menu. A hand appeared over the plasticised card and jerked it away. She looked up to see Louisa.

'Long time since we last met.' Louisa smiled, broadly. 'Lovely to see you after all these years.'

Her heart raced when she saw Guy standing behind her. He greeted her rather as a brother than an old lover. She appreciated loving just once was not a love affair. Perhaps he did not even remember what happened. Perhaps he was as drunk as she had been.

She studied him over the lunch table. If anything, she found him even more attractive, his hair slightly greying, his youthful lines had deepened. She felt his shoe touch hers so she sat with her feet under her chair.

They sat for nearly two hours talking about people they had known and their work, Guy a Broker, Louisa a television producer. A successful couple without children, although it was unclear whether it was by design or not.

Eventually, Guy stood up. 'I have to get back to the office,' he said, scraping his chair on the tiled floor.

He gave her a perfunctory kiss. 'It was nice meeting you after so long.' Then he turned to Louisa and kissed her lightly on the mouth. 'I won't be late home, darling.'

She stood with Louisa in a light rain outside the restaurant as he walked briskly away.

'I must be getting off as well, keep in touch. You have my telephone number?' Louisa asked, kindly.

'Yes, thank you. I will give you a ring,' she promised.

She pulled her raincoat across her body relieved she had handled the embarrassing situation well. At least as far as she was concerned. Someone touched her shoulder as she stood on the curb waiting for a taxi. She swung round. Guy was behind her. She said nothing as he gently moved her into a doorway.

His kisses were as she remembered them. She caught her breath as she attempted to push him away.

'Don't do this,' she whispered. 'Don't make me love you.'

He did not listen. Instead, he hailed a taxi and gave an address. The taxi stopped outside a tiny Mews house.

'My getaway,' he whispered, as he kissed her neck.

'From whom?'

'The world,' he answered, as he opened a yellow painted front door. 'I need a place to escape.'

'Does Louisa know?'

'Of course, she does. We use it when we go to the theatre or have dinner in town.'

'I am impressed.'

'I made a killing on the Stock Exchange.'

'Is there such a thing as a poor Investment Broker.'

'Only the ones with bad information or are caught with inside dealings. Wine?' he offered.

'No, I want to be clear headed. I want to remember what I did today.'

'Tomorrow is still twenty four hours away. So much can happen in that time.'

'War might break out,' she murmured.

'I want to savour peace now. With you.'

'Why after all this time?'

'Does there have to be a reason.'

'I think so. Nothing is for nothing.'

'Come and do nothing with me.'

She did not answer. War and Peace could wait.

*

'Why did you marry Louisa, you knew I loved you,' she asked, after their passion had subsided.

'I used her,' he answered honestly.

'How used her?'

'I worked in a bank, remember? Louisa's father could, how shall I say, improve my lowly position. Which he did.'

'And so you married her.'

'Of course.'

'You didn't love her?'

'Was that necessary?'

She got out of bed. 'Yes, I find that necessary. I also find it unfair.'

'Love with one does not exclude love with others. Come back to bed. Don't be so prissy.'

'So, my being here is of no consequence. I just happened to be around.'

'Of course not. I didn't mean that.'

'So, what do you mean? I am leaving. This was a terrible mistake. Keep away from me. I never want to see you again. Poor Louisa, what a lousy life she must have,' she said, pulling up her flimsy underwear.

'Actually, she has a marvellous life. Comes home any time of the day or night. No questions asked. Always some drama or documentary to keep her occupied let alone all the male attractions.'

'You have an open marriage,' she sneered.

'She chose for that.'

'I doubt it. I remember your wedding day or perhaps that was also insignificant. You were a toad then and you are an even bigger toad now.'

'It was not insignificant. I have not forgotten.'

'Well, please do and while you are forgetting it, forget now. I have wasted all these years thinking of you, putting you on a bloody pedestal.'

She ran down the stairs. 'I hate you. You can have no idea how much I hate you'.

He ran after her. 'Wait', he called. 'I didn't mean to sound like a playboy lover.'

'Say it as it is. You are a playboy fucker.'

It was dark when she arrived home. The lights were on and she could see Harry through the lounge window reading the newspaper. She felt sick with guilt and apprehension when she entered the house.

'Have a nice lunch with Louisa?' he asked, without looking up.

'Yes, it was alright.'

'Chewed over the past, I guess.'

'You could say that.'

'I have put the heating up.'

'Good, I am cold. You're home early', she added.

'Time to share some thoughts.'

'What thoughts?'

'You tell me,' Harry said, flicking the paper over to a new page.

'I'll start dinner.'

'Yes, let's eat early. I've asked some friends around for drinks this evening,'

'I have Steak is that okay?'

'Steak is fine. What did you have for lunch?

'Quiche,' she answered, choosing the heaviest frying pan.

'And Louisa?

She placed lumps of butter in the pan and waited for the heat to penetrate. She became aware of how long it took before the fat sizzled. It was, perhaps, the heaviest pan she had ever owned.

'Salad, tuna salad,' she called.

'And Guy?'

She froze. 'I forgot to tell you Guy came with her. How did you know?'

'An obvious conclusion. How is he?'

'Fine. He sends you his regards,' she lied.

'Is Guy still making a fortune?' Harry asked, as he opened a bottle of red wine.

'I guess so.'

'Why don't you ask them over?'

'I'll think about it.'

'I would like to see them again. I will give him a ring. Is he still working for those investment crooks?'

'Why do you say that?'

'If you make millions it's mostly at another's loss.'

'Is that so?'

'I think it is.'

'Then why see him again?'

'Perhaps he can give me a tip.'

'And that's okay, moral.'

'Moral! Ah, that is a subject to be discussed until death do us part. Love is blind,' he added, softly.

'Thoughts are free and I need a glass of wine.'

'It is said, wine is sunlight held together by water.'

'If you say so.'

'To us,' he toasted.

*

She had not intended seeing Guy again, not after giving his take on love and marriage. She regretted the afternoon with him and tried hard to love Harry the way he wanted her to love him and, whatever else, he was a good father and she could never consider hurting the children.

Guy phoned a few days later. She should have hung up but she wanted to hear what he had to say. She wanted to hear his voice again.

She tried to pull herself together, to use her brains, to remember what he said and how much he had hurt her. She made excuses how she could not get away so easily, how Harry would find out, not to mention Louisa. He was married. She was married. She recited every truth and near truth she could think of but he persisted. She knew he would win. She wanted him to win.

He opened the door immediately when she arrived at the Mews. They flew into each other's arms, undressing each other, leaving a trail of clothes to the bedroom.

A sexual encounter she had never yet encountered.

'I hate you,' she cried. 'I hate you.'

'That's good. It's raw emotion, that's good.'

'Shouldn't I say how much I love you?'

'I prefer hate to love. You can improve upon hate. Love is only a downhill track.'

'In that case, I hate you to eternity.'

Getting to the Mews every week was difficult and her excuses became more absurd. She knew Harry would soon become aware of her lies. She knew it was time to break with Guy or to ask his intentions but that was impossible since their liaison was too fragile and her fear of rejection too strong.

Strangely, cheating on Harry made her love him more and she thought he returned her love. Love born of guilt, she thought, hoping she might cover up her affair for just a little longer.

'Why are you suddenly so loving?' Harry asked, months later.'

'I don't know. I just see you as you really are. I love you for who you are. For what you are'

'Just as long as you don't hate me to eternity.'

'What is that supposed to mean?' she answered, sharply.

'Oh, my darling Felicity, you have been playing with fire. Now it is payback time.'

'I don't understand,' she lied.

'I would not have done it but Louisa did. Guy has been fooling around for years. She hired a detective agency to install cameras. Of course, they only record when there is movement. She said Guy has always had a string of women. She did not expect you to be one of them though she did mention her wedding day.'

'I am sorry. I was about to end it. I hate him.'

'Yes, I know.'

'What now?' she asked despondently.

'Louisa and I are thinking of starting together. She says you are welcome to him and all of his lies.'

'Let's try again. I love you more than Louisa does. I love you more now than I ever have before.'

'Convince me.'

'You want a good lay then I'll give you one.'

She could not remember all that she did but she thought it would be enough to convince him.

Eventually, she fell off his body, exhausted. He lay for a while with his eyes closed, smiling and perspiring.

'Guy has taught you a great deal over the past months, darling,' he said, meaningfully, as he stood up and dressed quickly. His tie hung loosely around his neck, his uninteresting light brown hair fell across his forehead and his grey eyes were now deep and piercing. No longer sad.

'You have hurt me for long enough.'

'I am sorry.'

'Don't be. I have been years trying to please someone that is not to please. At least by me,' he added.

He packed a small suitcase while she watched, crying.

'Please don't do this. I promise I will never see him again. I hate him,' she pleaded.

'Perhaps. I will be back for the rest of my things,' he said, coolly, as he left the house.

She stood in the open doorway with only her dressing gown wrapped around her and watched Louisa step out of a parked car.

'I knew the moment you met Guy you would begin your, not so secret, affair. You fell into the trap. I am surprised, it was so obvious.'

'He did it. He enticed me.'

'The blame game, darling,' interrupted Harry. 'I think you are a bit too experienced to be enticed.'

'The two of you began it now Harry and I will end it,' shouted Louisa, almost choking on her words.

'Harry loves his children. He will come back,' she wailed.

Harry turned to her. 'I am sorry but I will do my best to get custody. They cannot live with a child philanderer.'

'What are you talking about?' she screamed.

'Of course you don't know. Did Guy forget to mention it? It must have slipped his mind.' Louisa leaned against the car. 'I tolerated adult women but I had enough when he began with girls under eighteen. He had bad luck. One father took him to Court. Sixteen year olds look like twenty nowadays.' Louisa smiled, obviously enjoying the memory of his embarrassment.

'Oh, God, how could he, how could he. You can't blame me for everything,' she added, desperately. 'Your marriage was already over. Long before I came along.'

'My marriage was over before the Reception ended. It was not for you to screw my husband on my wedding day. That is unforgiveable.'

'Blame him. He did it. He has ruined my life.'

'Join the club, darling.'

'By the way,' added, Harry. 'It seems your love nest in the Mews is over. It was given to Louisa by her father so I don't think your friend will be using it anymore.'

Felicity sobbed as she told the police how Guy had come to her house. He was angry and aggressive. She told him to leave but he refused, pushing his way into her home. He threw her against a wall and began to rip her clothes. She had run into the kitchen hoping to get out of the back door but he caught her, pulled her to the ground and tried to rape her. She had managed to get away from him and picked up the first thing she could find which happened to be a frying pan. She had smashed it on his head. She did not think it would kill him. She just wanted to get away.

She wept as she told the Court that she had killed the only man she had ever really loved. She had killed the man she had loved the most.

It was, of course, Manslaughter. Her violent reaction to his attack was in no way premeditated. She received a suspended sentence especially as his wife, Louisa, told the Court how Guy had misused poor Felicity and many other women during their married life.

Louisa was happy with the Verdict. She considered Guy's death a release and certainly cheaper than a divorce. She really had to thank Felicity.

*

When it was all over, Harry returned to Felicity because of the children and, in any case, Louisa was never home. Her job took priority over all else.

Eventually, Harry and Felicity bought a farm on the Scottish border where they spent most of their days in 'wellies' and raincoats.

Louisa became an important Producer and married a Director of dubious films. Sometimes she even played a small roll. After all, she had years of experience.

# LOVE IN THE OLIVE GROVE

The telephone rang just as she and John had dozed off after Sunday lunch. It was Lucy, her younger sister by ten years. It was a surprise call since they had little contact. Almost none.

'Daisy, How are you?' Lucy asked.

'Fine and you. What a long time since we have spoken to each other.'

'I was wondering if you might like to come next week for coffee or tea, whichever you prefer.'

'Yes, of course, I would love to see you,' she replied, trying not to be suspicious of this sudden sisterly interest. 'Say when, I do very little these days.'

'Next Wednesday. Is that alright?'

'Wednesday is fine. I'll get John to bring me.'

'Well he can bring you but then he has to go,' Lucy replied in her usual abrupt manner.

'I'll tell him to 'bugger' off,' she laughed, knowing Lucy enjoyed a bit of rough talk.

'Before eleven. I have a nap most afternoons,' she replied still sounding as though it was all a bit of a bore, something she really did not want to do.

'Did you hear that, John? You may not stay, not even for a coffee. Just drop me off at her house and then 'b' off. Lucy is really something.'

She was shocked when Lucy opened her front door. She was almost unrecognisable, just a tiny frail old lady, her skin too white and parched, her blond hair now whispery.

She hardly dare ask how she was. It was obvious. Cancer had the upper hand and defied any physical camouflage.

She kissed Lucy's sunken cheeks.

'How are you?' she asked, because she could not think of anything else to say.

'Dying, Daisy'. Lucy smiled as if it was some kind of joke.

'I am so sorry, my darling.'

'Don't be. I have had enough of all of this. I want to tell you something before I am so drugged I cannot tell you.

They sat down in the lounge, the chairs looked worn out, especially the one that was obviously Lucy's favourite.

Coffee was in a thermos flask and a plate of plain biscuits strategically placed between two cups.

'I want you to remember when I came to live with you, so long ago. It is time you knew the truth,' Lucy informed her as she spilt the coffee into the saucer.

'What truth? There is no truth.'

'But there is. Edward, you and me.'

'Edward. What has he to do with it?'

Lucy closed her eyes and Daisy waited patiently until she opened them again.

'We were talking about Edward,' Daisy reminded her.

'It was so warm, the brilliant sun, blue sky and flowers.'

'What about Edward?' Daisy insisted.

'He came down once a month, in the beginning, later less often until,' her voice trailed off.

'Came down, where?'

'To the Olive Grove.'

'In Italy?'

'Yes, of course, in Italy, the happiest years of my life.'

'And Rick was he also happy?'

'He fell in love with an Italian woman,' she laughed, lightly.

'Why didn't you come home?'

'I didn't mind. I couldn't blame him.'

'How understanding of you,' Daisy replied, recoiling at the idea of accepting such infidelity.

'Do you remember how you worked for Edward?'

'Yes, I remember. I have never forgotten.'

'I did too. Remember?'

'Yes, I can remember you saying.'

'Well, that is it. Edward, you and me.'

'Oh, Edward,' Daisy whispered as she returned to her youth and first love.

Daisy adored him and he adored her. It was sad for as only son of the Managing Director he was totally out of her reach, out of her class.

Edward, named after his father and grandfather, became aware of his family's expectations and his position in life at a very young age.

He loved Daisy but he knew that any serious declaration of his passion would be foolish and that he must control any inner desires. Sometimes, he would stand next to her desk with some lame excuse so that he could bend over her, his body touching hers, his face just above her blond hair and she would glow, even perspire a little.

It was not long before the Head of Administration revealed this dangerous amour to Edward's father, out of loyalty, of course. In turn, the Managing Director's secretary informed the Head of Administration that Daisy did not work hard enough, nor was her work accurate enough. She must go.

Daisy had cried when she received her letter of dismissal and Edward threw the door of his father's office open demanding an explanation for his unfair decision.

His father had looked up from the pile of papers on his desk and clearly explained that he must do what society expected of him. He must marry a girl from a similar background and, hopefully, one that would bring new clients and money into the family business.

He was handsome and there were plenty of suitable girls. Edward as only son and the next generation of Smith and Smith would comply with his parents' wishes. He must accept that love was a nebulous state and understand that marriage was a case of mutual respect and duty. His wife must be socially acceptable and eventually produce an heir to carry on the family business.

After all, look at the royal family. He could not think of any one of them who was faithful to their wives and perhaps their wives were not as pure as the driven snow. Take Edward VI and so many others before and after him.

'Well, I am not royal and I want to marry someone I love,' he shouted, in defence of Daisy.

'You will do as we say. Get back to your desk.'

'Are you saying that you did not love my mother? Was your marriage one of convenience? Was she also a casualty of protocol?'

His father had become angry, angrier than he had ever seen him before. He reckoned he had touched a raw nerve.

He slammed out of the office. 'Get your coat,' he ordered Daisy. 'We are getting out of here.'

They had sat in a cheap teashop and Daisy had told him to go back. They could do nothing about it. Her life would be intolerable in his family. In the end, they would break them up. It was better if they did not see each other again.

Her heart broke when he finally agreed with her. She had foolishly hoped he would stand his ground but he gave in, perhaps too easily.

He had waited until the bus arrived then kissed her good-bye. She watched him walk away, back to the office. She had held back her tears until she got home.

She had married John, kind John. Of course, she loved him. Any woman would have loved him. A hard working ambitious young man working in the office of a large building company.

Daisy felt she was in seventh heaven. All her dreams had come true, two beautiful daughters and even a home help who came nearly every day. What more could she ask for. The answer to that was not her sister who arrived on her doorstep one evening with a suitcase. She and her husband, Rick, had a terrible fight. She thought they were incompatible. Her marriage was a terrible mistake and she would never go back to him. She was penniless and had no one to turn to except Daisy. Where else could she go?

Daisy was kind and accepted her sister's arrival with open arms. Lucy had always been treated as the baby of the family.

'My poor little Lucy. We will get you on your feet. Stay with us as long as you like.'

Lucy was an attractive girl also with blond hair, green eyes and a fair complexion but, after a while, Daisy resented her presence. The good night kiss she gave John, the little jokes they shared, sharing the bathroom and everything else which entailed sharing her home with a third party, even if it was her sister.

Eventually, she suggested to Lucy that perhaps she should find a place of her own. Her answer was vague. Always next week and John said nothing.

A few weeks later, Rick stood on her doorstep. He asked if Lucy was home. She told him she was working.

'I only want to know if she is okay.'

'Yes, she is fine.'

He turned to leave.

'Wait.' she said. 'I don't know much about her reason for leaving you but I do hope you can get back together.'

'I am sure we will, try not to worry and please do not tell her I came here. She will only think I am spying on her.'

'Well aren't you?'

'Not really. I am just concerned about her health.'

'Where are you working?' Daisy asked Lucy that evening. 'You have never really said.'

'A Solicitors office,' she replied.

'Where?'

'Near Bloomsbury Square.'

'Really. I once worked for a Solicitor. Which one?'

'Smith & Smith.'

'No, how is that possible,' she gasped. 'I worked for them ages ago. It was my first job. I was very immature.'

'Why do you say that?' Lucy asked.

'Because I fell in love with the son of the boss. He was way out of my league. I had the sense to walk away before I got too hurt.'

'That must be my Edward. He is about your age. His father had a heart attack and is now semi-retired. Edward has taken over.'

'How is he?' she asked trying not to sound too interested.

'I guess just as attractive as when you fell for him. Easy to love,' Lucy said, taking a lipstick from out of her bag. 'Bought it today. What do you think of the colour?'

'Did he marry?'

'Oh yes. Bitch of a woman.'

'Poor Edward.'

'Well, not anymore.'

'Why do you say that?'

'Because he is in love with me.'

'It is never good to break up a marriage. Any marriage,' she added, irritated by her irreverence to wedlock.

'It is already broken. So it is an open field day.'

'Well, let's hope you win the egg and spoon race. Don't fall and get egg on your face.'

'It is not about love, it is about keeping my job and getting as much as I can out of him before it ends.'

'But you have just said you are in love.'

'Yes, well. Love for his money. I did not say I am in love with him. He is in love with me.'

'I can't believe what you are saying.'

'Well, believe it. I am off to bed. Say goodnight to John.'

'Oh, Edward,' she whispered 'don't let this be true. Not with Lucy, I beg you, not with Lucy. I hate her,' she suddenly said, angrily and spitefully. 'I was not good enough and she is. I hate you both.'

Daisy lay in bed that night. She could not let this happen. Poor Edward, he must be desperately unhappy. Why choose Lucy, she had a common touch, loud talk together with loud clothes. Had his family's high standards fallen as low as her. She wondered if Lucy's failed marriage was not entirely her husband's fault. After all, being married to Lucy might not be a walk in the park.

She decided to get in touch with Edward. She could not contact his company, she might even get Lucy on the telephone and she had no idea where he lived. She would have to ask Lucy a few more questions.

She waited until John was under the shower before she started questioning her sister who was watching a late night film.

'How are the trains nowadays?' she asked, since there was a report on the news that night.

'Terrible.'

'Any point going by car?'

'None.'

'Well, what do the others do?'

'Grin and bear it.'

'And the Directors?'

'Well, if you mean Edward. He comes in about nine-thirty.'

'Where does he live?'

'In Surrey and that is all the information you are going to get from me, dear sister.'

'I was only curious.'

'Well, don't be. It is not your business where he lives or how late he comes to the office. You are not planning to see him again, are you?'

'Of course not. As I said, I am just curious.'

Daisy thought Lucy regretted telling her about Edward. She was right, she should have kept her mouth closed but, there again, that was Lucy.

Rick stood on her doorstep again next day.

'Come in', she said, hoping he was not going to make a habit of calling every day. 'Can I offer you a cup of tea?'

They spent over an hour talking. He was sorry that Lucy was angry with him. He loved her and he thought she loved him. He had a friend in Italy who owned a smallholding and olive groves. He had suggested he might come and help, perhaps for some months and he wanted to ask Lucy if she would like to come with him. She is working in a solicitors' office,' he added.

'Yes, I know. It is so coincidental because I worked there when I was young. My first job. That is a long time ago. I would like to meet Edward again but maybe it is better if I don't,' she gave a small laugh.

'A touch of 'unrequited' love?' he grinned.

'Sort of.'

He had left and promised to keep in touch and she hoped Lucy would go with him to Italy, have a few warm months together and return as happy as before.

She felt the tears running down her cheeks when she closed the front door. It was the first time she had cried since the day she and Edward had parted at the bus stop. She became aware of how much she had loved him and how much she still loved him.

'I have some good news,' Lucy informed her that evening.

'What?' she replied, as though uninterested.

'I have made it up with Rick and we are going to Italy together. We will probably stay for some months. What do you think of that?'

'Oh, I am so happy for you both. A new start. Fantastic.'

'I am going back to him tomorrow. He is going to pick me up around ten. We want to thank you for all you have done for us, for me.'

'What are sisters for? You were only here for a short time.'

'Long enough. I mean long enough for Rick and me to make it up and get back together,' she replied.

'We can message each other every day.'

'Yes, we will do that,' Lucy answered, sounding unsure.

Months later, it seemed to Daisy strange that she hardly heard from Lucy. It did not matter, she was always distant but somewhere she felt hurt. After all, she had stayed for more than two months with her and John. She supposed she was enjoying herself sitting under the Italian sun, drinking the local red wine and probably eating pasta cooked with a great deal of garlic.

If she did not have some contact messaging and sending small video films by mobile phone, she would have thought she had disappeared or was even dead.

She would just have to wait until she returned. After all, they could not stay away indefinitely.

They did not return for nearly five years. They looked well, tanned and heavier than before they left. She wanted to be overjoyed at their return but something held her back. It was as though they were acting a part, as though they held some secret. John, of course, did not notice. It took a woman's intuition to see things were not as they seemed.

Now, so many years later, she listened to Lucy's uneven breathing as she tried to explain what had happened. Her version of what had happened many decades ago.

'I did go to Italy with Rick.' She spoke slowly, one word at a time as though it cost her a great deal of energy.

'He harvested the olives and helped on the land while I harvested babies.'

She leaned back. 'What do you mean babies? You and Rick only had Mia.'

'I had more,' she whispered softly. 'Do you remember I worked for Edward? Edward Smith. Well, his wife could not have babies. So I stepped in.'

'What do you mean, you stepped in,' she asked, barely able to get the words out of her mouth.

'It was all terribly civilised.'

'What was civilised?'

'I stayed with you and John because Rick was against it. In the end, he gave in. We decided to leave when you wanted to look up Edward. His wife stayed with me all the time. It was all terribly civilised,' she repeated.

'I don't understand what are you trying to say.'

'I gave Edward and Constance a son and a daughter.'

Daisy breathed in deeply. 'When, when did you do that?' she asked, emotionally.

'The first three years Rick and I were in Italy.'

'What did you get out of it?'

'The olive grove, land and money. The land had been in Edward's family for years so when Constance told them she wanted to be alone and go to a fertility clinic, in Italy, her friends and family did not question her decision. I was telling you the truth when I said it was over money, not love.'

'And you found that okay?'

'I have just said it was a business deal.'

'You didn't want children of your own?'

'I wanted to keep the second baby but I had signed a legal document and it was too late. It would have meant Court cases and I could not do that to them or to Rick and me.'

'I can't believe it.'

Lucy gave a sigh as though relieved it was done with.'

'I guess his son was called Edward.'

'No, he was called Lucas.'

'After you, no doubt,' she almost spat the words out.

'Maybe. Don't forget I carried his child.'

'And the other child, what did they call her?'

'Constance, after her mother. Then, after they returned to England, I had Mia in Italy. Rick was the father,' she laughed and coughed at the same time.

'Well, I am happy to hear that.'

'Don't be like that. I did them a favour. Edward is the father and they knew who would be carrying their babies. It was all terribly friendly. Constance stayed with me all the time. She went back to London when I was three months pregnant. She said she was pregnant and came back here until the baby was six weeks old, after I had finished feeding. Then she returned here when Lucas was six months old and we did what had to be done. I was very fertile and could get pregnant at the drop of a hat, so to speak. Her friends might have guessed but if they did they did not say anything.'

Lucy closed her eyes again as though to recover from her long emotional story.

'I don't know if I could do that. I find you very brave and charitable.'

"'Well, we did well out of it. As I said, they gave us the Olive Grove. It was not about love.'

She left Lucy dozing in a chair when she finally left her house. She walked in a daze to where John waited patiently for her to return.

'You could have asked me,' she sobbed. 'I would have carried your baby. I would have given you a baby, with or without your wife's permission. You could have asked me, Edward.'

She no longer knew if she could bear to see Edward again, not after what Lucy had told her, but she needed some kind of a confirmation, closure was the name they called it now. She felt obsessed by Lucy's story. She could not let it go without hearing it from him, no matter how much it might hurt.

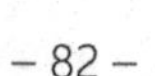

His office had been radically modernised, it was almost unrecognisable, his long legged secretary made her feel like a stodgy podgy old woman. She wished she had never come. It was a bad idea.

Edward kissed her on each cheek. 'Daisy, I can't believe it. How are you, what can I do for you. Come and sit down, what a surprise. Bring us some coffee,' he told his secretary.

He closed the door and she sat opposite him at his desk.

'My God, you still have the same desk as your father.'

'Couldn't get rid of it. It has too many memories,' he laughed. 'A couple of bad ones in between,' he hinted. 'Is there a reason for your sudden visit or is it a walk down memory lane.'

'A reason and a walk, a short walk.'

She told him Lucy's story. He shook his head while she was speaking.'

'Not a word of truth, not even a syllable, not even a letter. I have no idea why your sister should tell you this story. Perhaps, it is because she is ill and on heavy medication. We have a son and a daughter, both born in Italy. My wife, Constance, is their mother. I can find their birth certificates, if you really want me to,' he offered, sincerely.

'No, of course not. I should not have come,' she replied, feeling embarrassed. 'I guess it is a good reason to see you again. Have things gone well for you?' she asked, almost hoping he would say that he had made a mistake and wished he had married her instead.

'Yes, it has and for you as well, I hope.'

'John and I have two daughters.'

They talked for a while exchanging stories. Until he looked at his watch.

'Sorry, I have stayed far too long,' she said, standing up.

'I am glad you came. Take care. Who knows, maybe our paths will cross again.'

He gave her a light kiss goodbye, not the same kiss as when he had greeted her. It was noticeable, almost hurtful as though he was disappointed in her. She thought men were socially inept in these small details.

She walked down the old panelled staircase thinking how it looked just the same as all those years ago. She thought little had changed except for the modernisation of his office and Edward, of course.

Edward who now had receding hair, the beginning of a paunch, puffed around the eyes, perhaps from too much alcohol, and a few hairs straggling out of his nose and ears. The handsome Edward was no more than the average middle-aged male. She was certain he saw her in the same light. A middle-aged plump woman. What a mistake to remember people as they were and not as they are now. She regretted spoiling his memory of her and her memory of him.

*

'That was easy,' she thought, as she sat in the train going home. He had not been shocked or angry but brushed Lucy's story aside as he turned their conversation on to some other topic. Looking back, he did not even admit to knowing Lucy in London let alone the olive grove in Italy. He had not even asked after her health. He was in denial of ever having known her.

She did not believe him. She believed Lucy who on her deathbed had to tell the truth to someone who loved her. Now, she saw things differently. Edward's carefully picked wife could not give him a son. What a disappointment to his parents. He must have felt a failure. His wife must have felt a failure. How difficult it must have been for both of them to face his father, a man who lived in a time capsule. A man unable to progress into modern times. She even felt sorry for Constance and for Lucy who must have made numerous visits to an Italian Fertility Clinic. She thought it must have been traumatic to carry two babies only to give them away at birth. Daisy thought Lucy had probably done it for Rick who had lost his job and was deeply in debt.

She turned on her side and watched John sleeping. She could afford to love him, unconditionally. There were no ghosts between them anymore.

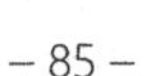

She received a call from a Hospice informing her that her sister was now coming to the end of her life and wished to see her one last time. She left immediately and John offered to drive her and wait in the Lobby, perhaps with a cup of tea or coffee, if he was lucky.

She bent over Lucy as she tried to say something. Her voice was now barely audible.

'I loved Edward', she whispered. 'I gave him babies. They were my babies not hers. I was their mother. She had no viable eggs.' She gave a hint of a smile. 'It was better than being a secretary.'

Daisy's voice trembled as she asked, once again, if Edward had loved her.

'He never stopped loving you. I thought you should know. He once told me that he could only make love to me if he pretended I was you. You can imagine how I felt. That is why I kept away from you.'

'Where is Mia?' she asked, trying to change the subject.

'Where she always is. In Italy with Rick and the love of his life.'

'You didn't divorce.'

'The woman was Catholic. She was married and couldn't divorce and we never got around to it.'

Lucy closed her eyes though she was not asleep.

'Is Mia coming?' Daisy asked, as she considered the absence of Lucy's only child rather unkind if not disturbing.

'I don't know,' she murmured. 'She never forgave me for the other babies. She has a short memory. She has forgotten we did it for money. I did it for love and money. I saved Rick from bankruptcy. So easily forgotten.'

'You told Mia?'

'That devil woman of his told her. The Bitch.'

'Of course she did. I hope she and Rick rot together in hell.'

'Maybe I will be there first,' Lucy grinned as she closed her eyes.

Daisy thought she might wake up again but she never did.

She left the Hospice crying but not for the loss of Lucy.

# RETURN OF THE HIPPIE

Joanna considered her life to be extraordinarily boring. At least she found it so. Sometimes she allowed herself the luxury of regretting what she had not achieved. She knew she should be grateful for all she had but she was not.

She had lived rough in a hippie commune, in California, and demonstrated against the Vietnam War and supported the equal rights movement. She had been, in fact, a persona non grata but she had managed to avoid the police, though occasionally it had been a close shave. Perhaps, that was why love and close relationships had been important. She wondered if the hippie movement would ever rise again against war and the misdistribution of wealth. She actually thought she would like to return to those days. An old hippie supporting peace and justice while listening to the sound of a guitar and air filled with the unusual smell of cannabis.

However, tragic events had overtaken any plans she might have had to lighten up and try to obtain a Green Card, a work permit, so that she might stay in paradise, or so it had seemed at the time. She had returned home and been persuaded, mostly by her mother, to stay. After all, a sports car was an incentive at the best of times. She had not wanted to settle down, not wanted to catch the 7.58 to London and sit in a grey office behind a black typewriter.

Now, suddenly, 'out of the blue', she had an unexpected visit from an old hippie friend, Gus. He had been, in fact, more than a friend. He looked almost the same, his now grey hair still tied back in a ponytail, light blue jeans, a shirt and a pseudo leather jacket. Stained brown suede shoes completed his casual outfit together with an untidily cut beard.

He had brought with him a small plant from the Salvia family, in place of the usual bunch of flowers or box of chocolates.

'Does this remind you of something?' he chuckled, as he placed the colourful pot on her windowsill.

'No, should it?'

'Perhaps not this particular plant but others like it.'

'What is so special about this one?'

'It comes from Mexico, does that give a hint?'

'It must be a drug?'

'You bet but don't try it. It gives an immediate high and can frizzle your brains. Anyway hallucinations.'

'Must I be happy to have it in my house?'

He grabbed her arm. 'I just thought it might bring back some memories.'

'I would rather forget the most of them. Would you like a cup of tea?'

'Have you something stronger. I want to celebrate our continued friendship. Let's hope it will be as intense as before.'

She laughed. 'How intense do you think it will be?'

'As intense as you like.'

Gus had stayed longer than she had expected. In fact, they had sat up all night remembering evenings spent around campfires, smoking pot, singing and loving. Love had seemed so uncomplicated in those days, perhaps because there were no parental boundaries, no jealous girlfriends since everyone loved someone. Just pure, unguarded freedom.

They had laughed at their careless relationships and she told him how she still had a couple of long dresses and beads in a suitcase in the attic. She kept the conversation light avoiding the reason she came home when she did. Avoiding Caroline.

He told her how he had married an American girl but she was unable to have children and had left him after ten years of marriage.

He returned to the U.K. since he had not become a U.S. citizen. He never heard from her again. He had not re-married but she guessed he had women enough.

'She blamed me,' he told her.

'Why, why were you to blame?'

'Said I gave her something.'

'What something?'

'She never said.'

'Then she should not have accused you.'

'Those were the days, my friend. I thought they would never end,' he sang.

'But they did and here we are now in 'those black titanic hills.' Not hills, but mills',' she added, doing justice to the poem. 'I am beginning to feel depressed.'

'Life should be seen as a challenge. Like a race,' Gus said, reflectively.

'Luckily, I have yet to cross the finish line.'

They talked to the early hours of the morning until eventually they crawled, in their clothes, under the duvet.

'I also couldn't have children,' she murmured.

He did not answer. He had fallen asleep.

*

She woke up next day, in the middle of the day. Gus was standing next to her bed with a cup of coffee in his hand.

'Oh, God,' she moaned. 'Look at the time?'

'Is someone waiting for you?' he asked, grinning.

'No, not that I can remember.'

'Well then it doesn't matter.'

'It is a matter of principle.'

'To hell with principles,' he said, falling on top of her.

'Get off me,' she said, pushing him away. 'That is not going to happen.'

'Want to bet?'

'Yes, because I'll win.'

'We laid together in bed last night. That was okay, wasn't it?'

'Yes, you warmed my cold feet.'

'I could make you warm all over.'

'Wishful thinking.'

'I'll be off,' he said getting up. 'I have to meet someone this afternoon. See you tonight.'

'I can't remember inviting you.'

'Neither can I but I will be back anyway.'

*

She had taken a step back by the time Gus arrived. It was all too quick, too personal, even if she had been intimate decades ago. In fact, she could hardly remember much apart from the campfires, the cannabis 'joints', the free love. Only one emotional happening was still clear in her mind. She had always tried to avoid thinking about the last month of her stay. She had cried nearly all the way home in the plane. She had found it strange that her mother, perhaps even her sister, had not guessed her pain. Why should they? They did not even know Caroline had existed.

She would ask Gus tonight, perhaps he might know what happened, exactly what happened. After all, he was part of that particular group.

She and Gus had a quiet dinner, it was as though the first enthusiasm had subsided and the realisation that their youth was of the past and anything now was just clinging on to what was in bygone days.

Perhaps he did not feel as she did but she only knew that she had to straighten out the past, that night.

Gus was lying along her couch when she came in with the coffee. She recognised the smell of cannabis.

'Still enjoying a 'joint'?'

'Want one?'

'First my coffee. I have not puffed for ages. I am not sure what affect it will have on me.'

'Now is the time to find out,' he suggested as he sat up and held his hand out to her. 'I have a feeling you are worried. Come and sit next to me.'

'I suppose I am,' she replied. 'Your turning up has made me think of Caroline. Not that I have ever forgotten her.'

'Yes, that was a miserable time but she knew what she was doing.'

'I doubt it.'

'Everyone thought it.'

'What?'

'Well, it was a bit of a coincidence, she had just broken up with Mitch.'

'What are you suggesting?'

'That she took an overdose on purpose.'

'Why should she do that?'

'Don't know,' he replied, obviously lying.

'Where did you go today?' she asked, reacting to a gut feeling he was hiding something.

'Actually, I met Mitch. We had a beer together,' he added.

'That is coincidental, you visiting me while you are seeing Mitch. Do you meet him often? Tell me, what does he do now? I want to hear everything.' She stopped. 'But first I have some rather good brandy. Would you like a glass with the coffee?'

She had one thing in mind and that was to get Gus either drunk or drugged or both. Only then, would he disclose anything he knew.

'So tell me', she said, handing him more than a double brandy.

He swirled the brandy around the glass, inhaled the strong aroma and sipped it.

'This is a good one,' he said, as though he was a connoisseur.

The mix of cannabis and brandy made him quickly talkative, but at the same time sleepy.

'Well, you know how it was,' he slurred. 'Something was bound to happen.'

'Such as?'

'Well, Mitch and I used to bet.'

'On what?'

He laughed. A sort of arrogant laugh.

'On you and Caroline and the others, of course.'

'What was the bet about?' She could feel herself become not only nervous but, unusually, aggressive.

'You don't want to know.'

'But I do. Tell me, it was so long ago it no longer matters.'

'Well, we used to bet on which of you girls slept with which boys and for how long.'

'Okay,' she answered slowly as though giving herself time to digest what that meant. 'If I remember correctly, I was only with you for a couple of weeks and then I stayed with Jason until I had to go home.'

'Yep, I earned ten 'joints' a week. If I could keep you for over a month then I got a bonus of fifty.'

He laughed, obviously finding it amusing.

'And Caroline?' she asked, trying to keep her voice light.

'What do you mean?'

'You said she took an overdose. Caroline was mad for Mitch. She told me he had promised to go back to the U.K. and settle down with her.'

'Never heard that before.'

'I would like to ask Mitch myself.'

'He won't tell you anything.'

She filled his glass again while he rolled another 'joint'.

For a moment, she thought he might fall asleep. She shook him a little. 'You were saying?'

'About what?' he queried.

'About Mitch and Caroline.'

He was by now well under the influence of drink and drugs.

'Well, it was all a bit of a joke. I told Caroline about the bets Mitch and I were placing. Of course, she did not believe me and ran off to ask Mitch. She chose a bad time because he was 'high' and admitted to what I said. Stupid girl. She broke with him and the next thing we knew she was dead. That's why I query what she did.' He took another mouthful of brandy. 'So unnecessary. She could have known Mitch was not serious.'

'You killed her, both of you killed her.'

'If you say so, darling. Come here and give me a kiss.'

She glanced over to the plant. 'The kiss of death,' she whispered.

She patted his face. 'Something else. What did you give your wife to make her leave you?'

'Gonorrhoea, what else.' He frowned. 'It could have been the one with a 'C'. Don't know anymore.'

'Chlamydia?'

'Could be. That rings a bell.'

She winced. Her two weeks with Gus were life changing.

He slept on the couch. She thought herself rather kind when she threw a blanket over him but, there again, she did not want him to catch a cold. She had some cooking to do. She thought he might appreciate a nice Fruit Cake.

He woke up, hours later with a headache. She gave give a Paracetamol and invited him to stay the night. He thanked her and asked if he might once again share her bed. She said that was all right just as long as he did not have any ideas.

Of course, he had ideas but she managed to keep the situation under control until he fell back to sleep. It was all a bit of a game only he could not know it was deadly.

She did not sleep. She was too busy thinking about Mitch and poor simple Caroline who believed the promises of a hippie. She had tried to make a collection to help bring her home but the hippie community had little to give and Caroline's family were poor. In the end, she paid most of the costs and flown home with the coffin. She met the heartbroken family at the airport and stayed with them until after the funeral.

She had tried to console them by suggesting Caroline had a problem sleeping which made her depressed. Somehow, she had got hold of a bottle of Valium and taken too many. It was a tragic accident. All her friends in California were devastated and sent her family their condolences and love.

She had cried when she eventually took the train home arriving to the surprise of her family who showed signs of irritation that she had not warned them of her imminent homecoming. She had smiled and played the part of the prodigal daughter.

*

She walked over to the sunny windowsill where he had placed the Salvia plant. She did not know anything about this plant but she did know how to release ingredients from the leaves of other plants.

Strange how things work out, she thought. If Gus had not come by, she would never have known the reason behind Caroline's death. It seemed unbelievable that Gus and Mitch were responsible, no matter how harmless it might have seemed at the time. Then there was the problem of the letter 'C'.

She insisted Guy went home after breakfast and she would visit him in his two-roomed flat.

*

Two days later, she plied him with numerous slices of Fruit Cake while she ate two slices of Sponge Cake.

She left early owing to the heavy traffic and took the remains of the Fruit Cake with her, just in case some visitor fancied a slice or two. She sung as she drove back home, she no longer considered her life extraordinarily boring.

She hoped it was the last thing Gus ate before he became muddled. Permanently muddled.

It was some months before Joanna saw Gus again. He was standing at a Bar having a drink with a balding man wearing a pair of dark rimmed glasses. It was not Gus who interested her but the man. She was sure it was Mitch though it was difficult to be certain.

She pushed her way through the crowded Pub until she stood behind the rather heavily built man. Gus saw her immediately.

'Hi, Jo, haven't seen you for a time.'

'True, I have been away, staying with friends. But I did bring you a Cottage Pie before I left, remember?'

'Did you? Oh, yes, I remember. I shared it with the cat.' He roared with laughter.

'Thanks for that.'

The man turned around. 'Not Jo. What a surprise Gus told me he had met up with you. How are you?' he asked, in his usual jovial manner and kissing her lightly on both her cheeks.

'What are you doing nowadays, Mitch?'

'Debt Collector.'

'That sounds depressing.'

'Sometimes.'

'Why don't you and Gus come round for a cup of tea and I'll make my special Fruit Cake? Do you remember, Gus, you put away quite a few slices.'

'How could I forget? What cake was it?'

'Fruit Cake.'

'Oh, yes, I remember. I was sick after you left. It was too rich for my stomach.'

'I am so sorry to hear that,' she answered trying not to sound disappointed.

'But it could have been from some left-over fish I had for lunch.'

'Let's hope it was the fish,' she muttered.

Gus said he had to take 'a leak' and she and Mitch stood at the Bar together.

'How do you think Gus is?' she asked, pretending to be concerned with his health.

'Not too bad. Sometimes he is a bit depressed. That is why he looked you up. Sometimes he takes something to help him feel better.'

'What's he on?'

'Mostly cocaine, cannabis and whatever he can get hold of.'

'I often think of Caroline,' she murmured.

There was a short silence.

'I do too,' he eventually replied.

'What exactly happened?'

'The usual, drugs.'

'I thought she died of an overdose of Valium.'

'Same thing, drugs.'

'She told me you had a fight with her or rather you told her your relationship was not as serious as she thought.'

'Did she tell you that?'

'Yes, she did.'

'Not true.'

'What is true then?' she asked, trying to control her obvious dislike of him.

He did not answer since Gus returned. He wiped the back of his hand under his nose.

'Had a sniff?' asked Mitch.

'Yep.'

'I was just talking about Caroline,' she said.

'Still busy with her death. What's your problem?' Gus asked, aggressively.

'I do not have a problem other than it was a trauma that I have never recovered from. Neither of you took her coffin home. Did you, Mitch?' she asked, accusingly.

'Nope, that was not my scene.'

'You mean facing her family was not your scene?'

'That's woman's stuff.'

'Macho. Eh?' she replied, disliking both men even more than before.

'Leave it alone,' said Gus, sniffing his wet nose.

'What is there to leave alone, after all this time?'

There was a strained silence. It was obvious that neither men wanted to talk about Caroline.

'I find you a coward, Mitch. You were her boyfriend. At least she thought you were. Why else would she have taken an overdose of Valium? She was a very balanced person. I find it difficult to believe she did that.'

There was the usual silence as they closed ranks.

'I have to be getting back to my party.'

'I will be waiting for my Cottage Pie,' called Gus.

'Not if you give it to the cat.'

'Only kidding.'

*

She was walking to her car when she became aware of someone behind her. She held her car keys tightly in her hand prepared to push them into some man's face but it was a young girl. She sighed with relief.

'Sorry, I didn't mean to scare you.'

'I am not so easily scared,' she lied.

'Can I talk to you for a moment?'

'Do I know you?'

'No, but I know Mitch and Gus.'

'There is a small café over there,' she suggested.

They walked over the car park in silence until they entered a café full of jute boxes and young people.

'There is a place over there in the corner,' she said, taking off her thick scarf before ordering two cups of tea along with two wrapped sandwiches.

'I haven't eaten,' she explained. 'Would you like one?'

'No thanks.'

'Okay, what about those two imbeciles?'

'I heard you talking about Caroline,' the girl whispered.

Jo gasped. 'What about Caroline?'

'Mitch lives with my mother. She wants him out but he won't go. He and my mother had been drinking heavily one night and I overheard Mitch telling her about his hippy days. Nothing new, but then he began talking about this girl and how she died.'

'Caroline?'

'Yes, Caroline. It seems he and Gus were 'high' and wanted Caroline to take part in a ménage à trois. You know a threesome. She refused so they put Valium in her drink.'

'You heard him say this?'

'Yes, I was disgusted because he found it amusing. What I gathered, she was so drugged they did what they wanted. Next morning they found her dead.'

'Nothing surprises me. Then what did they do?'

'They cleaned her place up. Took their prints off the bottle of Valium, put it in her hands and placed a half a glass of water with only her prints on it, even smudges from her lipstick. Then later, they pretended to find her.'

Jo sighed. 'I wish I could be shocked but I am not. The autopsy showed she had intercourse before she died. In fact, they killed her by giving her an overdose of Valium. Just for sex.'

'When I heard you say how you had brought Caroline's coffin home, I sort of snapped.'

'What low lives. I guess there is nothing we can do or prove after so long. I hate them.'

'I know something about Mitch.'

'What', she asked, hoping to nail him in some way.

'He deals.'

'In drugs?'

'Yes, and I know when the next delivery of cocaine arrives. He will get a long prison sentence if they catch him with it. I want to tell the police but I am dead meat if his supplier finds out I have told on him. That is why it is dangerous for me, or my mother, to report him. We need an outsider.'

'You can make an anonymous phone call.'

'I am too frightened.'

'I will have to think about it.' She frowned. 'Where were you standing in the Bar so that you could overhear our conversation?'

The girl did not reply to her question.

'The delivery is next Monday evening at eleven thirty.' She stood up. 'Do what you want. You won't see me again.'

'The address, I don't have the address.'

'The police know of him. You don't need the address.'

She finished her tea and sandwiches before leaving the noisy café. She glanced around at the youth and wondered where and what they would be doing in the future.

She wanted to scream 'be careful, life is full of false best friends.'

She now had to make one of the biggest decisions of her life. Should she believe the unknown girl and, hopefully, revenge Caroline's death or just walk away from it all. Should she make a dangerous moral decision or play it safe.

# THE WOMAN WHO SPOKE TO JESUS

Tiny Mrs. Munroe looked lost in her long hospital bed that stood in a separate room for terminally ill patients. A male nurse stood by her bed, smiling down on her. She wanted to smile back but her mouth did not seem to move in that direction.

'How are we this evening?'

She wanted to laugh and ask him whether he meant the 'Royal We' or perhaps he meant a 'wee'. That took her back to her childhood. She wondered what had happened to all that time. All those years had passed and there was so little to show for it. A lost husband, brother and two sisters. She tried not to think about it.

She supposed she would see them again though she was unsure whether Wilf would really want to meet up with her after sixty years of bickering marriage. She was herself unsure if she really wanted to meet him again.

The male nurse was now washing her. She did not want this young man striping her clothes away and touching her where he wanted. She tried to fight him off but he only called another nurse who held down her thin fraying arms.

Modesty, a patient's whim, was ignored and to be strictly controlled with a hard hand, a physically hard hand.

There was nothing she could do but to accept it and the inevitable consequence of a too long life.

Someone, from some church, had visited and read something from the Bible. She could not remember what it was except it made her cry. She had felt small tears running down her sunken cheeks. The middle-aged woman had held her hand and said how Jesus loved her unconditionally and was waiting for her.

She had continued to cry even after the kind woman had left and a pretty probation nurse from the Philippines had come and whispered how it was true, Jesus did love her.

'But he does not know me,' she thought. At least, she could not remember meeting a young man with that name and she certainly could not remember sharing a bed with him. There were others who she had been intimate with, but not one with that name.

It must have been night when she woke up. A light from the corridor lit her room. She found that restful. She liked the night. It was when she spoke to those she had not seen for decades, her siblings and her mother who still called her 'Chickilik' or 'Fairybell'. She could still sit on her mother's lap, a comfortable full lap, while she mended her childish broken heart when teased at school; comforted her when her best friend was not her best friend. Now, her mother soothed the pain of her being a mind without an obedient body.

A new doctor entered her room. She stared at him through her half-closed watery eyes. She thought perhaps he was from some eastern country and had not yet realised he must wear a white coat as all the other doctors did. She thought the hospital management should be stricter with the 'imported' staff who were not wholly qualified.

She regretted that she could not rebuke him, give him a piece of her mind, but she was unable to form words.

The doctor smiled but said nothing, only his clear brown eyes penetrated her thoughts. She turned her head to face the wall. She did not want to feel uncomfortable with this young man. He should say what he had to say and then leave her alone.

She thought that he spoke to her yet she did not hear him speak and his garment was uncannily white, whiter than her sanitised surroundings. She wanted to ask him which washing powder gave such a translucent glow.

She glanced down at his feet horrified at his sandals. Surely, that was not allowed, not even a pair of socks donned his rather long brown toes. She really did not know what to think of the modern generation.

Then, he did the most extraordinary thing. He moved nearer to her bed and held his hand over her forehead. She felt fear and to her relief a nurse arrived.

'I can give you something if you can't sleep,' she offered without acknowledging the man next to her bed.

She wanted to ask her who was this 'import' doctor but, as usual, no real words left her lips.

'I'll be back in a moment,' the nurse said, which actually meant a good half an hour, if not longer.

The new doctor spoke again. 'I sent for the nurse to help your fear.'

She wanted to tell him to just go away, get lost. In fact, a rude word beginning with a 'b' entered her mind but she managed to dismiss it before he, the import doctor, read her thought.

He smiled a very special smile. 'You have to get up and tell them.'

'As if,' she thought.

'You can do it, if I tell you to do it.'

'I've had a Stroke. I cannot move or talk. I am waiting to die,' she thought.

'I know. That is why I have come but you have first to tell them.'

'Tell them what?'

'That I am here.'

'What is your name?'

'Jesus.'

'The woman said you love me.'

'Yes, I do. I love you all.'

'Even the Ward Sister?'

The night nurse was angry when she returned. Mrs. Munroe was sitting on the side of the bed. She was even searching for her slippers.

'What are you doing? Get back into bed at once or I will call a doctor'

'He has just been. Didn't you see him? You should have done, you stood right next to him.'

It occurred to the night nurse that Mrs. Munroe was talking and moving around rather erratically.

'Here, take this. It will make you sleep. We will discuss this tomorrow.'

'I have to tell you,' she said, just audibly.

'What do you have to tell me, Mrs. Munroe?'

'Jesus has been. He has healed me. See, I can talk and move again. He says he is here. He didn't say where he was going to,' she frowned as she slurred her words.

'Yes, of course. I am happy you are feeling better. Just take your pill and tomorrow we will walk around the Ward.'

The night nurse wrote her notes.

"Mrs. Munroe was extremely restless. However, she sat up unaided and could talk to some small degree".

Unfortunately, Mrs. Munroe did not survive the night. The doctors thought that perhaps the Stroke was not as severe as they had thought and it was possible that she could still move and speak a little.

*

'Who's that bloke?' asked a hospital security guard sitting behind his screen.

His counterpart turned his swivel chair. 'That's film from yesterday, look at the date, mate.'

'How come the screen shows yesterday while the cameras are on now? What's he doing there at twelve at night?'

'The night nurse seems to be ignoring him.'

'Strange garb he has on. Looks like a Roman senator. We did Julius Caesar last term at school. I was a bloody guard.'

'Roll the film back. Look, you can see him enter the room, about three minutes later the nurse enters. She leaves and returns about ten minutes later. Then she leaves the room again after five minutes.'

'Look at this. There is nothing on the film until a nurse enters the room at five-thirty. Then, she runs out and another nurse goes back into the room with her. Then a doctor enters. They close the blinds of the window to the corridor and then they all leave closing the door behind them. The man never left the room. Where is he? Where did he go?'

'Go back to when he enters the room. Look at his feet.'

'You mean his sandals?'

'Yes, but not only that, it looks as though his feet are not touching the ground.'

'Get away with you. That's only how it looks.'

'Roll back the film again. Now look.'

'It's too unclear.'

'No, it's not.'

'Yes it is. It must have been okay otherwise we would have heard about it.'

'I have to report this.'

'Think before you do. We'll look like a couple of assholes if we are wrong.'

'I will look into it by myself. I'll start with that night nurse, she must know something.'

'Perhaps he was a relation.'

'He did not leave that room and I want to know where he went. You never know he might come back again.'

'Yea, there is something fishy about him. What day is it?'

'Monday. Yesterday was Easter Sunday.

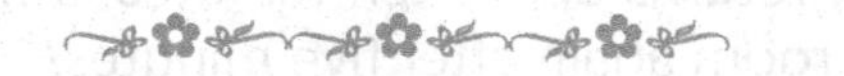

# ANYONE FOR BRIDGE

Sally was not one of them. Not one of the clique who considered themselves a cut above the others who lived on an estate a few miles away. Her lack of social inclusion diminished her self-confidence and that led to her lack of insight when bidding or, worse still, when playing. In fact, the small elite Bridge club saw her as a weak link in their strong chain of friendship and their high standard of play.

Of course, Sally understood her lowly position and tried to compensate her shortcomings by plying her friends, not real friends, with an assortment of superior cakes and biscuits when it was her turn to have them home. However, this only gave the old biddies something more to criticise on their way back to their perfect residences.

It seemed Sally was doomed to stay an outsider. Her fragile position 'hung by a thread' for should a newcomer arrive, and happen to be of some importance, then she would be replaced without disturbing a hair on their neatly permed judgmental heads.

She had seen this degrading and humiliating decision played out before, leaving the ousted player destitute of self-esteem and confidence for most of their remaining years.

The situation worsened when Charlene, who flaunted her expensive clothes and jewellery, joined their Bridge club.

She thought Charlene had invested in a facelift for her red lips had a strange tight look; thinner than a rather fatty crayon but thicker than a pencil line. However, she had to smile when Charlene wore too short and too full summer frocks and skirts, exposing most of her aged legs when climbing the stairs.

She had to admit that she held herself well, better than most of her elderly friends. Straight upright posture, no sign of a Dowager back and rounded shoulders. Perhaps that was why she was confident enough to display her summer legs. Sally thought there was no reason to like her.

It was Sally's turn to be the Hostess and she pondered on how she could make their lives uncomfortable. She had heard how Caraway Seed cake could make the consumer feel happy and Poppy Seed in bread and cakes could leave small signs of opiate in the body.

She decided to make a Poppy Seed cake with a more than generous sprinkling of seeds on the top.

The members of the Bridge club arrived and, to her surprise, they brought a bunch of flowers with them. This she thought was the prelude to her dismissal. She would try to pre-empt them, she was not about to be humiliated by a bunch of self-serving nobodies.

'We thought a small gesture might help.'

'How kind of you,' she gushed. Help what?'

Bridget, the bringer of good news or bad tidings, shuffled her feet as though running away was an option or even her shoes were too uncomfortable.

'Charlene can be a bit undiplomatic. We thought she might have upset you last week.'

'I did not think anyone noticed. We all have to do what we are told.' She tut-tutted as though she were a stern schoolteacher.

The group, which had now enlarged to six plus Sally, shuffled into her cosy lounge. Chintz curtains fluttered in the light summer breeze and matching settee and armchairs completed the very county 'twee' look. She thought it harmonised well with the neighbourhood in which she lived.

Charlene, who did not tolerate any other opinion other than her own, made her usual 'here I am' entrance.

'Attention, please,' called Charlene, to the chattering women. 'We wish to broaden our horizons by increasing our membership so that we can compete against other Bridge clubs in this area. Perhaps we might even hire the village hall once a week. It is a good beginning if we can get together around six tables, twenty-four Members.'

'Do we know so many people who play Bridge in this area?' Sally asked, amazed at this news and surprised she was still a member of the club and wondering who were the 'we'.

'As you might know,' Charlene continued, coldly ignoring Sally's remarks. 'We want to encourage people from the other side who play Whist and are willing to take a few Bridge lessons. You have to take what you can get,' she sighed. 'You can't always choose.'

'What do you mean, 'from the other side'? Are they dead'?

'Sally, don't be so difficult. From the estate, of course.'

'But they won't want to play Bridge with us.'

'There are some who want to improve their lot in life,' Sylvia interrupted, supporting Charlene.

'I don't see how playing Bridge with us will improve their lot,' Sally mumbled, rebelliously.

'No, but it will enlarge our club.'

'I think it is a case of us wanting them and them not wanting us.'

'Sally, you are not listening to what I am saying. We are simply trying to expand the club. We might, one day, if we have enough players, become members of the Bridge Bond. That is our aim. Has anyone anything they would like to add.'

There was a hushed silence.

'Who agrees with Sally,' asked Charlene, intimidatingly.

No one answered. After all, Charlene had managed to become the Chairwoman of the unelected committee within a couple of years. Sally thought that was rather clever since other members had been playing for so much longer and considered themselves to be happy before she informed them otherwise. However, dismissal to the fringes of local society was not unheard of and Charlene appeared to be a powerful woman, one not to be crossed.

'Motion passed,' stated Charlene.

'You are not the Chairman of a committee meeting. There is no Motion to be passed,' Sally interrupted. 'You don't even have a gavel to keep order.'

'Chairwoman,' corrected Charlene. 'And you are out of order. We need new members and there are none around these parts,' replied Charlene, sharply.

'Fine, I hope they will come and I hope we can make them feel at home, here on the other side of the track.'

There was another hushed silence.

'I will put it to the vote again,'

'What again?' Sally retorted.

'Sally, be quiet or get out.'

'I would if I could but I happen to live here.'

'Meeting adjourned.'

'What about our afternoon?' asked an irrelevant member of the Bridge Club.'

'And I made a cake for nothing,' complained Sally.

*

'I have to introduce Shelley,' said Charlene, trying to sound upbeat in a negative atmosphere some weeks later. 'She is one of the new members of our club and we hope she will enjoy Bridge and all the friendships attached to it.

The other new members are having extra lessons for a couple of weeks longer but we can begin with a trial run this afternoon,' continued Charlene. She lifted her hand rather as royalty does when waving. 'Have a nice afternoon everyone.'

Sally turned to Shelley who looked extremely flashy in her cowboy boots, mini skirt and a leather jacket with bling-bling diamond studs. 'Would you like to play with me?'

'I thought she should play with Jeanette,' interrupted Charlene, considering Sally's suggestion as interference.

'No, thanks, I am happy with Sal,' replied Shelley.

'I have never been called that before,' laughed Sally, enjoying the thought of an interesting afternoon.

'I know of you, my friend does for you.'

'You mean Chrissie?'

'Yea, she says you are real nice to work for. Did you know she and Debra have won their fight against the Council.'

'Which fight?'

'They have been years lobbying to get the new housing estate built, just down the road from where you live. My hubby and me have other plans,' offered Shelly without disclosing what they were.

By the end of the afternoon, she and Shelly had scored the most points.

'Beginners luck,' Shelley concluded.

Sally did not believe a word of it since Shelley shuffled the cards by dividing the pack and flipping them through each other at a speed she had never seen before. She was not what she seemed, not quite the simple card player.

*

It was when summer drew to a close did Shelley drop a bombshell.

'The girls and I want to thank you so much for having us here. I have such good news. Cause of how you being so kind to me, my hubby has bought a house here.

We was planning to move away but I says to my hubby that I want to stay here. I have so many friends on the estate but also here in this lovely club. We have bought the old house opposite you, Charlie.'

Charlene shuddered at the shortening of her name.

'We are going to have it demolished and build a real Hollywood type house with a swimming pool that is half in the house and half in the garden. And a tennis court,' she added, proudly. 'Then, when it is finished, we are going to hold a blooming big BarBq.'

'You must have a lot of money. How come you live on a housing estate,' asked Charlene, sarcastically.

'My husband began a small casino, all legit,' she grinned. 'And I help him. Learned a lot about cards and people.'

'Is that fair, playing here?'

'Of course it is. Just a bit of psychology. Just 'cause we come from nothing does not mean we're stupid. What is more, the girls and me are starting our own

Bridge club. And we won't be drinking boring cups of tea but glasses of the good old bubbly.'

She turned to Charlene. 'You're welcome to join us, Charlie.'

Sally thought Charlene might faint for she seemed to sway, her skinny body succumbing to emotion.

Everyone rallied round except Sally, of course.

'I would love to play in your club if you have a partner for me,' Sally asked, excitedly.

'You are all welcome. We could just as well play by me, in my super new house, than in this dusty stuffy village hall.'

Everyone agreed. They would all like to join Shelley's club. They would play Bridge in the village hall until the super modern house was finished. Then they would all park their German and other expensive cars in Shelley's long drive. Some of them even hinted they might wear a swimsuit under their polyester frocks.

Sally sat back amused. They had constantly criticised their new members and now, suddenly, they were best friends with a young woman from the 'other side'.

'What a flock of sheep,' she muttered. 'They follow whoever has the most to offer.'

At least, Charlene had lost her place. She supposed that was good news.

*

It was eighteen months later when the members sat on stools around a bar in Shelley's new shiny kitchen. They had played cards and, as was now the routine, taken a swim before going home. Two champagne bottles stood on the bar and Sally and Charlene had disappeared to the Ladies room, at the far end of the pool.

When Sally eventually left the Ladies room to join the other women, she noticed billowing material above the water. It was one of Charlene's many full-skirted frocks and Charlene was hanging in its folds. She stared for a moment undecided what to do. She could not help her unaided and if she was resuscitated then she might have brain damage.

She was aware of wasting valuable seconds. Her most primal instinct was to walk away but she knew that was impossible so she screamed for the younger women for help. Three of them sprung into the water and dragged Charlene to the side, heaving as they pulled her up the steps and laid her on the tiled floor.

Shelley began to push down on her chest while Brigit called for an Ambulance. Suddenly, Charlene opened her eyes and Shelley fell back onto her heels, shaking with emotion.

*

Charlene said she was unsure what had happened only that she had used the Ladies room before going home. She supposed she must have slipped on the wet tiles because the next thing she knew she was in the pool. She admitted she was a little giddy after the second glass of champagne. She vaguely remembered seeing dear Sally but after that nothing. She would have drowned without Sally's quick reaction to her desperate situation.

Happily, Charlene was no longer the same woman since she had seen a light at the end of a tunnel, her husband was there but he pushed her back. Whether it was a 'near death' experience or not did not seem to matter. She was eternally grateful to them all, especially to Sally who had found her and Shelley who had resuscitated her.

Some days later, she whispered in Sally's ear that she was sorry for all the things she had said. Sally told her it was a pleasure saving her and she would do it again, if must.

*

Sally felt rescuing a woman she intensely disliked was more than an act of duty since Charlene had found God and went to church every Sunday.

She thought Charlene's spiritual experience erased the need for her to repent for any sins she might have committed, especially the sin of pushing the dominant half-drunk into the pool in the first place.

# THE DEMISE OF THE DINOSAUR

Her dinosaur still stalked the earth, it controlled her every move and she had retaliated, when younger, by secretly shopping and hiding the illicit goods under the bed. Then she would wait for the occasional sexual encounter, mostly unsuccessful, when she took the opportunity to show off the new frock or perfume.

The perfume was easiest to own up to since she saw it as foreplay, though it did not necessarily guarantee a mutual climax.

Waiting for the bank statement to arrive on the doormat was not an option.

She thought it strange that most of these cumbersome necessities, husbands, died before their partners though it was a fact that dinosaurs became extinct while the meeker weaker species of creatures crawled under a stone and survived.

However, her dinosaur still plodded around and spent most of its wearisome life in the garden or slouched snoring in front of the television with its flabby paunch hanging over its trousers.

Sometimes, it gave a little shudder as though it had lost its breath but, to her disappointment, it always recovered. The worst was when it farted forcing her to open a window while she went upstairs to recover. Even worse, was in bed. She had made the excuse that he snored which was true but secondary to his awful bodily release of air. She had happily moved into the second bedroom.

The dinosaur seemed quite oblivious of its habits and she was too polite to draw attention to them. After all, she supposed that was how dinosaurs always were. It was just a leftover from millions of years ago.

Since companionship had become an obsolete word, she had settled for the occasional outing with the Women's Institute. These outings had become her only contact with the outside world excluding, of course, visits to the local supermarket or a gossip with the neighbour.

She felt it was time to take things into her own hands and the dinosaur must become extinct. It had lumbered around for long enough taking up her time, energy and the earth's oxygen.

The dinosaur who had been a sports enthusiast, though now its body barely showed any sign of its youthful activities, insisted staying each year at a secluded hamlet on the south west coast of Cornwall. It was off the beaten track, existing of little more than a few holiday rentals and a popular Pub that attracted other holidaymakers from a somewhat larger village further down the coast.

The steep path and steps to the beach were not only a deterrent to parents with young children but to everybody else who could think of better places to stay. That was exactly what attracted the dinosaur even though she had to struggle up to the top of the cliff, stopping every few feet to catch her breath. It was not that the dinosaur did much better but it saw this as a yearly challenge if only to prove it was still fit and, of course, the rental of the cottage was considerably lower than elsewhere.

'A penny saved is a penny earned', was his adage every year.

She had tried to suggest other possibilities to the dinosaur but it refused any routine that might disturb its equilibrium. It seemed her womanly needs were of no importance to this overbearing carnivorous freak of nature.

They had arrived at the cottage on time and she had unpacked the suitcases, had an early dinner at the Pub, that was also a yearly ritual, and immediately afterwards retired for the night. After all, it was a long way to drive.

She lay in bed staring up at the ceiling, hoping that tomorrow's climb up the steep path would be her last, or nearly her last. She was unwilling to wear out her knees and hips, sacrifice her body, for the whim of a dinosaur. She would not hear its grunting and snoring or slobbering one more day or night. Tomorrow, it would disappear into the outgoing current, forever lost at sea.

She had planned its demise some time in advance by saving two sleeping pills from months before. She finely crushed them and poured the powder into a small pillbox and hidden it until she packed for their holiday. Her plan had to be well timed. Timing was of the essence, of the utmost importance.

The holiday routine was just as unremitting to change as the daily routine at home. Breakfast, shopping perhaps at a local market; return home; drink coffee on the patio; walk a little way along the cliff path; have a light lunch and eventually make their way down to the beach.

The dinosaur would then walk to the sea, dabble its feet and return to where she sat on the dry sand, her back against a rock. It was not comfortable, never had been, but she always did what the dinosaur expected.

Now, today, she could only hope that the routine followed its normal course, that the weather stayed fine and that the dinosaur went swimming.

So far, all was normal. The dinosaur had a light lunch along with a glass of milk spiked with two finely ground sleeping pills. She thought any white residue from the powder would be less noticeable.

It drank the milk without comment and sat back in a comfortable chair while she hastily washed up, scrubbing its glass fanatically just in case there should be any obscure police investigation.

'Shall we go?' she called. 'It's a pity to miss the sun.'

'I don't really feel like swimming today. I think I will give it a miss.'

'Rubbish, a quick dip will tone your muscles, freshen you up. Just in and out.'

'Perhaps you are right,' it agreed, standing up and stretching his ungainly body.

They made their way to the top of the steep path. Unusually, the dinosaur walked behind her but she had no time to query this small change of habit.

'I feel rather giddy,' it complained.

'We are almost there,' she replied, encouragingly.

*

There was no easy way to get there for the dinosaur slipped and fell onto her, she in turn toppled and together they fell down the path and steps, it crashing on top of her at the bottom of the cliff. It was rumoured that her death was instantaneous. Crushed by the weight of her husband.

The dinosaur laid in bed for two weeks reading travel brochures and planning a luxury holiday or two.

The hospital assigned him a Dietitian and his girlfriend promised to keep him on track. She visited him every day since they had both lost their partners and the Women's Institute had lost one of its most reliable members. They had so much in common.

# THE RED SPORTS CAR

Leo stood on the steps of his parents' house and stared at the small red sports car standing in the drive. He remembered how it was a gift from his parents on his eighteenth birthday and how he drove it with the panache of a young handsome bachelor.

He walked down the steps, opened the small door and stepped in. The keys were still in the lock.

'Why not,' he muttered, as he turned the key and revved the old engine. It gave a familiar splutter before it slowly moved away.

It seemed he knew where he was going, it seemed as though he drove without having to concentrate. He found it odd but accepted how it was.

He stopped about five miles further down the wooded lane and turned right into a long drive with lawns on either side.

A girl was sitting on a stone garden bench. She stood up as he slowed down.

'I have been waiting for ages. What took you so long?'

He sprung over the low door of the car.

'I don't know. I suppose I overslept. I am sorry. Is there anywhere you want to go?'

'Silly question. You know where I want to go.'

He wanted to ask how he would know but said nothing. He wondered if he was in a dream and would wake up in a panic, sweating, though he could not really see why he should be in a panic. Everything was very quiet, unusually quiet. Even the sound of birds was missing.

The girl got into the car and he drove away, her white scarf blowing romantically behind her in the wind as she turned on a rather ancient radio.

'That's an oldie', he remarked.

'How can you say that? It is the latest hit.'

'Is it. Oh, well, you can see I know nothing.'

'Only that you love me and want to marry me,' she teased.

Leo flinched because he knew that this afternoon had to be one of honesty.

He stopped the car.

'Lizzie, you know I have to accept this job. It is a chance of a lifetime. I have to take it. You do understand, don't you?'

'No. I don't understand. There are plenty of jobs here. You don't have to go abroad.'

He squeezed her hand. 'I do Lizzie. I really do.'

'How long will you be away?' she asked, tearfully.

'My first posting is for three years.'

'Take me home, you bastard. You knew you were going away. You knew that before,' she stopped.

He denied he had completely known his plans before they had made love. He did love her but not enough to give up his chance to go abroad.

Of course, he felt bad. He knew he had taken advantage of her He knew he should do the decent thing and marry her but his desire to leave was stronger than any social correctness.

They drove home in silence.

'Wait,' she said, as he was about to drive away. 'I have something to show you.'

She ran into the house and came out a few minutes later with a bundle in her arms.

'Look, isn't she beautiful?'

'Yes, whose is it?'

'Ours.'

'What do you mean by ours?'

'Yours and mine,' she answered, proudly.

'Okay, joke over.'

'It's not a joke. She was born six months after you left me.'

'I left you over thirty years ago.'

'No you didn't. You left and came back because of our baby.'

He placed his hand on his forehead.

'Lizzie, you aren't making any sense. This is a small baby and we are thirty years down the road.'

'Look in the mirror,' she said, moving the car mirror towards his face.

He saw himself as a young man.

'See you came back to us.'

'I have to go,' he said, unable to understand what was happening.

He glanced once more in the mirror. He was not young, he was middle-aged and his hair was grey.

'I'll be in touch,' he shouted, as he pressed his foot on the accelerator. The tires threw up the fine stones on the drive leaving small skid marks as she ran up the steps into the house, crying.

He knew he was waking up from a nightmare, a strange dream, a bad film that he had once acted in and forgotten his lines. Forgotten how it ended. He wanted to return but was frightened to do so. Frightened to see the pain he had caused. He was aware of Marianne standing next to him.

'Wake up, Leo. You have to take your pill.'

'I don't want it. It gives me bad dreams. Take it away.'

'The doctor says it will help the headaches'.

'I get nightmares. I don't want it.'

'Do it for me if not for yourself.'

He sighed. He did not want to be difficult. In any case, he secretly hoped his strange nightmare would return. It was intriguing to dream of his first real girlfriend.

He hoped she had met someone who loved her. He knew that would be easy if only because of her wealthy family.

He could feel the yellow coloured pill working. He hoped it could take him back to the small red sports car and his lost youth. He hoped he would find out what happened to Lizzie and her baby. Not his baby, that was for sure.

*

The sports car was still standing outside his parent's house. He looked around the grounds and walked into the hall.

He called, 'Mum, Dad', but there was no answer so he walked back outside into the dazzling sunlight. He was once again aware of the stillness, no sound of a gardener mowing the lawn, no sound of dogs barking, no sign of swooping birds. He wanted to leave this deserted country house. He wanted to find Lizzie.

Lizzie was waiting as before on the garden bench. She stood up exactly as before

'I have been waiting for ages. What took you so long?'

He sprung over the low door of the car.

'I don't know. I suppose I overslept. I am sorry. Is there anywhere you want to go?'

He was aware that they repeated the same conversation, listened to the same song, drove down the same road.

He was aware that they were in a scenario of past events from which he feared he could not escape.

He drove her back home as before.

'Wait,' she said. 'I have something to show you.'

She ran into the house and came out a few minutes later with a bundle in her arms.

'Look, isn't she beautiful?'

He could hear himself screaming. He could hear her screaming but not from where she was standing with the baby but further away, somewhere far away.

*

'Wake up, Leo,' Marianne was calling. 'You are having a bad dream again.

He could feel Marianne shaking him but he did not want to wake up. He wanted to return to Lizzie and his past.

'I must ask the doctor about these pills maybe he can give another prescription'

'Wait until his next visit.'

'Are you sure?'

'Yes, I am sure.'

He laid back on his now puffed-up pillows and thought of his dream. A dream of instalments, each time revealing more. He accepted there would not be a good ending. He had not expected there would be one.

Marianne came back hours later with an assortment of pills. The large yellow pill was not there.

'Where is the yellow pill,' he asked, trying to keep his voice even and unemotional.

'I thought you shouldn't take it,' Marianne replied.

'I will decide that.'

'They upset you.'

'Give it to me. The doctor will decide, not you.'

He knew he sounded ungrateful, even cruel.'

'Whatever you want. I can't do any more than I do.'

She sounded unhappy but he could not care. He wanted to return and only the yellow pill took him to where he had to be.

*

The red sports car still stood in front of his parents' house. He called them but, as before, there was no one at home. He wondered where they were. Surely, they could not always be out.

As before, he drove the short distance to Lizzie's house but Lizzie no longer sat on the stone bench but stood outside her parents' house while her father neatly fitted suitcases into the back of his car.

Her mother cradled her against her full breasts. 'I will come as soon as I can.' She turned to her husband. 'Drive carefully, dear. It is a long drive to Hamilton. You really should have gone by train. Don't forget to give Rosaline my present and my love.'

'I'll stop off in Birmingham on the way back and do some business with Tom Philips,' her father replied.

Lizzie's mother kissed her child's curly hair. 'I will 'phone every day. Try to help your aunt as much as you can. I will come any time you need me but I can't get away for a while.'

She hugged and kissed Lizzie until she stepped into her father's car.

'No one will know, I promise you that, Lizzie. No one will ever know.'

Lizzie wiped her streaming eyes 'Please come as soon as you can, please Mummy. I am so sorry.'

Leo felt a pain, Lizzie's pain. 'Wait', he shouted as the car drove down the long drive. 'Wait, I'll come with you.'

The car did not stop but turned left along the road with rows of now stark leafless trees.

He turned and walked back to Lizzie's deserted house.

*

He woke. Marianne was standing next to him.

You are dreaming again. What is your dream? Leo, tell me, perhaps I can help.'

'I think I am already in Hell, Marianne'

'Of course you aren't. Tell me, who is Lizzie? You call out to her every time you are asleep. Who is she?'

He could see Marianne was near to tears and probably thought he had some past affair.

'It is so long ago,' he sighed.

'Tell me, Leo. Tell me what happened, I have to know.'

He told her what he knew about Lizzie, who she was, where she had lived. How he had left to work abroad. No more than was necessary because Marianne did not have to know Lizzie was his first love.

Marianne stroked his hair and said it would be all right. He would eventually stop dreaming about her. It was only a phase caused by the medicines. She would read to him until he fell into a natural sleep.

It was not a natural sleep for he was standing outside a stark stone house. The wind swept around its cold grey walls while lights were burning in almost every room.

Screams came from within the house but he dare not enter, he dared not face the event that was taking place within. He was a coward.

An undertaker's car drew up. The men, dressed in black, drew a tiny white coffin from the back and carried it into the house.

Lizzie appeared by the front door when they eventually left carrying the small casket. An older woman held her tightly as she sobbed, uncontrollably, and rested her head against the coffin and kissed it, delicately kissed it. The men walked slowly, reverently, to the waiting car as Lizzie gave a heart-rending wail when it disappeared behind the closing door.

He thought he would die of pain, not the pain from his cancer but the pain of the one he had loved and left and the pain of his lost child.

He broke down and cried as he had never cried before.

*

When he returned he saw only his room with a table full of bottles and necessities for a sick person.

'Marianne, where are you. Marianne,' he called almost hysterically.

He could hear her running up the stairs. 'I'm coming, I'm coming,' she called.

She sat on his bed. 'Did you dream again?'

'Yes, I have to return. Lizzie needs me. My pills, give me my pills. I have to go back.'

'You must first eat something. I have made some chicken soup. Please try just a little.'

'Then will you give me my pills?'

'Yes. I promise.'

*

He had driven Lizzie back home, as before.

'Wait,' she said. 'I have something to show you.'

She ran into the house and came out a few minutes later with a bundle in her arms.

'Look, isn't she beautiful?'

Once again, he could hear himself screaming. He could hear her screaming but not from where she was standing with the baby but further away, somewhere as far away as Scotland.

*

'Leo, I have a surprise. You can't imagine who has come to see you.'

He turned his head to see an elegant woman next to his bed. He frowned as he tried to recognise who it might be.

'Leo,' she said softly. 'Remember me?'

'Lizzie?'

He looked at Marianne. 'How did you find her, how did you find Lizzie.'

Lizzie laughed. 'Not difficult since I still live in the same house as before.'

'I never dared to look for you. I felt so guilty.'

'Is that why you dream of me?' she smiled, lovingly.

'I keep dreaming of you. I thought you had died and was punishing me.'

Lizzie smiled at Marianne. 'I am still alive and kicking though my husband might be better off without me.'

'Who did you marry?' Leo asked, curiously.

'I went to University and met Ralph. You don't know him.'

'I am happy it all turned out well for you. I am so sorry you lost our baby.'

He heard a sound of gasping followed by an almost indiscernible cry.

'How do you know that?'

'In my dream. You lost a little girl, in Scotland. I was there when they took her away in a small white coffin. You came to the front door and kissed it. My dream was so sad.'

She stood up quickly. 'I have to be going. Ralph is waiting outside in the car.'

She bent over and kissed Leo on the cheek. 'No more dreams, promise me that.'

He held her hand. 'I know what happened. I was there.'

Lizzie sat in the hall before she went home. She looked obviously shocked and Marianne offered her a glass of water but she refused. Ralph was waiting in the car. She was just a bit shaken up. She would be all right in a minute.

'What did Leo say that upset you?'

'Everything.'

'I should not have asked you to come.'

'No, it's good I came. I just do not understand how he knows so much. Only my Aunt Rosaline was with me. She might have talked to my mother but no one else and my mother would never have gossiped. Not to anyone. His dream was true. I went to my aunt in Scotland when I was three months pregnant. I lost my baby three months later. No one could see I was pregnant when I left here No one knew I had lost a baby when I returned. No one knows I stood at the front door and kissed the tiny coffin. Only Ralph knows I lost a baby but I never told him I went to Scotland.

Leo broke my heart,' she whispered, almost inaudibly.

'If it is of any consolation, Leo has been through hell and back. He has a brain tumour and he says the medicine makes him dream. Now, at least, he can die peacefully. Thank you for coming.'

'I called my baby Leontine. We buried her in the grounds of our house. That is why I could never move away. I guess Leo's soul has already found his daughter.'

# HAPPY NEW YEAR

Belle had known it was unwise to sell her house to her son and his wife but they had promised to build an extension. She could live in what they called a 'granny flat'. A contradiction, in terms, since they were childless. They said they would take care of her for the rest of her life and she would never be lonely or lack any creature comforts. She would have money in the Bank and no other responsibilities. What more could she ask for? She thought the answer to that was more money than they were prepared to pay for her house.

She stared out of the window at what used to be her garden and thought of her husband, Charles, who had taught Latin at a private school only five miles away.

'Do not despair, 'Nil desperandum'. You only have to find the right key to fit the right lock. Everything is solvable,' he would say when she worried over something.

'The key to my own house was the right key,' she mumbled.

*

'You must understand,' Helen said, kindly, as she handed her a cup of tea. 'We are also getting older. We need to move to something smaller, more compact. We will find you something you like. You will always have the last word. You don't have to take anything you don't like.'

'It's my house. You promised I could stay until my last breath. You promised me that.'

Helen sighed. 'I know we did, dear, but we would like to travel, feel free, and not have to worry about burglars or whether you are safe here alone.'

'You don't have to worry about me. I am perfectly capable of looking after myself.'

'Maybe now, but think of the future. We thought we could find you an apartment. Perhaps even in the same area as us, even in the same Park.'

'The garden is so beautiful, just look at the white branches of the trees.'

'Please be reasonable.'

'Would you mind driving me to the library, I need a couple of new books.'

'Let's go down to the cottage,' suggested Rob after dinner that night. 'We can spend New Year there. The lake will be frozen, I'll take my skates.'

'What about your mother?'

'What about her?'

'We could take her with us.'

'You must be joking,' he answered.

'No, I am not. We should sweeten her up, promise to take her with us when we go away. She has never been down to the cottage in the winter.'

She smiled as she studied the lights around the frozen fishpond and wished Belle would trip, crash through the thin ice and drown in a couple of inches of water.

'That's very magnanimous of you,' he answered, after swallowing a mouthful of brandy. 'You don't have to do it to please me.'

'I do it for Belle,' she replied, as she now pictured the hard banks of the lake and the ice only broken by the reeds in the shallow water.

She would take Belle for a walk then hurry home on some pretext while Belle conveniently slipped into the icy water. At least, that is how it had to look. Difficult, she thought but everything was possible, all that was necessary was the opportunity and the right timing. Rob skating too far away to see his miserable mother nosedive into the slushy muddy shallows

She could not allow this selfish old woman to win, not for endless years. She did not think she needed to feel any remorse.

Belle sat silently in the back of the car between the duvets and pillows. Her thermal underclothes protected her against the excess cold but, most importantly, her bottle of Sherry stood safely in her shopping basket.

Helen, on the other hand, was talkative and lively. Rob frowned, somewhat amused, wondering why his wife should be so elated. After all, his mother was sitting in the back of the car and that was enough to depress anyone, let alone Helen who was a depressive by nature.

*

'Shall I let her sleep in?' queried Helen, as she spooned powered coffee into mugs, next morning.

'I am already up,' called Belle, as she carefully made her way down the open staircase and walked towards the all-burner stove. She glanced at a pile of wood stacked in the corner.

'You have been busy.'

Rob looked up. 'Brought it in last time we were down here. If I don't do that then it will never burn well.'

'So thoughtful, just like your father,' Belle sighed.

'I have never thought of Rob being like your husband. Interesting,' grinned Helen.

'They say,' continued Belle. 'It is the woman who makes the man.'

'Really, I will have to remember that.'

Rob zipped up his padded coat and hung his skates around his neck.

'I am going out, see you later,' he informed his wife and mother, sounding bad tempered at their silly conversation.

'He has not changed a bit,' twittered Belle that evening. 'He is still the same schoolboy I remember.'

'Have another glass of Sherry, dear,' suggested Helen. 'You know, I think we should go home tomorrow afternoon when Rob has finished skating. It is too cold here,' she added, having given up the idea of getting Belle out of the cottage and along the slippery banks of the lake.

'I was hoping you would say that,' Belle agreed, sounding relieved. 'It is already dark, where is he?' She pulled the curtain to the end of the track. 'He should not stay out so long, he should be back by now,' she murmured, recalling the numerous times she had said that when he was a child.

Helen opened the front door allowing the icy air to sweep through the warm cottage.

'I think they are having a party over there,' she remarked. 'There are flashing lights.'

'What's going on?' asked Belle.

'I'll go and have a look. Perhaps he is having a drink with those new people. Don't forget it is New Year.'

'That is very selfish of him to make us worry. I can't believe he would do that.'

Helen pulled on her fur lined boots and ski jacket. 'You had better hope he has. I won't be long.'

She stamped her way along a known track now hidden by snow and pulled her scarf across her mouth to lessen the cold air.

Apprehension overwhelmed her as she realised the lights were from an ambulance and police car.

Two young police officers walked towards her.

'Are you missing anyone, Madam? There has been an accident.'

She knew, instantly, that the male skater who slipped at speed under the ice was Rob. She listened to how other skaters were unable to reach him and there was no sign that he had surfaced. She gave a Statement after which she told the young officers how his mother was over in the other cottage and she really must get back to break the dreadful news.

Belle was sitting in front of the wood stove when she arrived home, rocking to and fro and, at the same time, sobbing as though in time with her movements. She hardly needed to hear the details for she seemed to know that she had lost her only child, her only son, her reason for living. Then, suddenly she stood up and staggered, wailing, into the bright night; sliding on the icy track; recovering and falling again and again while at the same time crying, 'Oh, Rob. Oh, my Rob.'

A faint moon and a few bright stars were still shining in the cold morning sky. Normally, she would have stood gazing up at the beauty of the universe considering the force of creation. Now, seven hours later, she walked quickly to the edge of the lake. She glanced around the banks and called Belle several times. There was, of course, no answer, no movement between the leafless trees. Only an unrecognisable form laid heaped in the reeds.

The police were still present and she gave them yet another Statement. She could only assume Belle had left the cottage sometime in the night. Maybe, she was searching for her lost son. So tragic, so sad.

*

Months later, she walked out onto the mooring and stared across the lake. Rob's death had brought with it a degree of freedom and she really did not see the point of saving an old woman who would grieve for the rest of her life. After all, you put an animal down if it is in constant pain.

# THE DECORATOR

GLoria looked out of the window at the raindrops coagulating on the smeared glass. Clouds darkened the already sombre house, probably built in the early nineteen hundreds, consisting of a narrow hall that led to a front room, dining room, scullery with a door to the garden and a tiny room behind the scullery. This was the only room facing west catching the late afternoon sun. Her favourite room. The dining room should also have received a few golden rays but a large trellis and hanging grape vines blocked any light from entering.

Various tenants had painted the woodwork, coat upon coat, and the last coat chosen was bright blue, perhaps peacock blue. She had tried to cover it with a cream coloured paint but the blue was not to be so easily defeated and broke through wherever and whenever it could. Then, there was the wallpaper, layer upon layer. She wished she had a strong man to help but there was no one and the children were too busy, though they always had time for video games.

*

'That's what I am going to do,' Neils informed his mother and sister.

'What?'

'Find out who I am.'

'You know who you are,' laughed Viv.

'Look at those people on the television. They did not know anything about their dead family. Maybe, we have a dead someone who was interesting.'

'I very much doubt it,' replied Viv.

'You are so boring,' he sneered.

'No, I am not. What do you think, Mum?'

'I think you will find only names and dates.'

'What did your father do? You never talk about him,' asked Neils, sounding curious.

'That's because he died when I was young.'

'And your mother?'

'She died as well, young.

'Is that why you went to live with Aunt Sarah.'

'Yes'

'What happened to her?'

'She died.'

'Why did we never meet her?'

'She moved away and we lost touch.'

'Don't you have any cousins or anyone else in the family?'

'No'

'Wow, you have a really boring background, Mum.'

'I told you, don't waste your time.'

'I'll see what I do,' answered Neils, defiantly.

Ten days later, he flapped a piece of paper in front of her face.

'See, Mum, I have sent away for your birth certificate but I can't find your marriage certificate. Where did you get married?' asked Neils.

'Not here.'

'Where then?'

'Iraq, before the war started. That's why you can't find it and never will.'

'And you say our family is not interesting? So where is my father now?'

'He was killed out there.'

'Why is his name not on our birth certificates?'

'Because, at the time, I thought it might endanger you. Some of his own people saw him as a traitor.'

'Why were we born here?'

'I have just told you, because of the dangerous situation out there.'

'And your marriage is not registered in the U.K.?'

'No'

'Is that not unusual?'

'No'

'Where did you meet him?'

'In a restaurant.'

'What did he do?'

'He worked for the British army.'

'Doing what?'

'Translator'.

'Wow, that's cool.'

'It looks it me as though we are illegitimate,' added Viv, sounding depressed.

'So what if you are,' Gloria snapped.

'I have to digest this,' Niels muttered.

*

Ahmed had been so incredibly handsome and she had fallen in love. Head over heal in love. They had lived together, on and off, for five years during which time Neils and Vivian were born. He had promised to marry her when the war was over but he never returned from one of his missions. That was why she did not move away from where she lived. Perhaps he would return, perhaps he was not dead. After all, she had not officially heard that it was so. She was not his wife, not recognised by either the Iraqi or the British government.

She had simply received a small letter, more of a piece of paper, in the post saying that Ahmed would not be coming back to Britain. He had disappeared, presumed dead.

She had cried, for days she had cried until Neils and Vivian began to ask the reason for her unhappiness.

She had struggled on, always living on the edge of poverty. She did not regret the children but she did regret the naivety of her youthful love. She had wanted to believe every word he said, believe his promises, but now she questioned the truth.

It was some months later when an odd job man called at her door. He could fix anything and was, at the same time, a painter, even a plasterer.

She had asked him the usual questions such as where was his company and where had he worked before. She had found his website on her laptop and even contacted his past clients. He seemed genuine enough and he offered her a price she could not refuse. He would paint the woodwork throughout and rehang the wallpaper downstairs and even promised to steam off all previous layers that, she thought, still held the smell of boiled cabbage.

She had given him the spare front door key so he could let himself in. She really had nothing to steal and any jewellery she had she took with her to work. The children promised to come home together so they would not be alone with the Decorator. She was very careful about those kind of things.

The Decorator was halfway through the job, or at least, the walls now showed their original ugliness and the paintwork rubbed down to almost the original wood. She was extremely happy with the foreign looking Decorator, who she thought had an Italian background.

Her conversations with him were mostly over what he had done that day but eventually she asked him where he came from.

'Iraq'

'I knew someone from there', she said, softly.

'Yes, I know you did.'

She gasped. 'How do you know that?'

'Your friend used to come to the same restaurant as my friends and me. An Iraqi restaurant, of course.'

'That was years ago,' she said, sadly.

'I suppose so.'

'He was betrayed and they killed him.'

'So they say.'

'Do you know anything about it?' she asked, hopefully.

'No more than you know.'

'Do your friends know anything?'

'I am certain they do not.'

'Can you ask them again to be sure?'

She left the room feeling that he knew more than he was telling. A feeling of anxiety ran through her. A feeling that something bad was about to happen.

Later that evening, she mulled over the coincidence of the Decorator knowing Ahmed. It seemed a little too unlikely. Too good to be true. Not that there was anything good about it. On the other hand, the few Iraqi's in the area would stick together in a close-knit community and it might be possible they had met each other years ago.

The telephone rang.

'Gloria?' a guttural voice, asked.

'Yes' she replied, carefully.

'I have to see you, I need help.'

'Ahmed?' she asked, breathlessly, as the caller hung up.

She ran upstairs, took a quick shower and dressed in her newest frock. That and a good layer of makeup and perfume completed the effect she wanted.

It seemed ages before she heard the front door key turn carefully in the lock. Of course, she thought, Ahmed would still have a key.

She ran down the narrow passage ready to fall into his arms. To hold him, kiss him. No matter the reason for his absence. She stood expectantly but it was not Ahmed, it was the Decorator.

'What do you want,' she asked, nervously.

'We will wait together,' he said.

'I don't know what you are talking about,' she replied, trying, unsuccessfully, to push him back.

They were by now in the lounge and she had tried to grab the phone. He took it from her.

'Try to keep calm. Nothing is going to happen to you.'

'The children are upstairs, I'll scream.'

'I would not do that if I were you.'

'What do you want?' she repeated.

'I have told you already, we will wait together.'

'What for?'

'Your husband, who else.'

'My husband is dead, you know that.'

'You are my bait. I am sorry but we have tapped your telephone. We know he is coming here tonight.'

'Please don't hurt him. We have children, please don't hurt him,' she sobbed.

*

Niels could not sleep, partly because of the heat and partly because of the heavy smell of oil paint. He walked over to the window and breathed in the warm moist air. It was then he became aware of his mother's lowered tone along with that of a man's. His mother had not mentioned a visitor so he crept down the stairs avoiding the creaking treads. The door to the lounge was slightly open so he was able to stand and listen, unseen. He was amazed to see the Decorator sitting with the telephone on his lap telling his mother to stay where she was and wait with him.

His first impulse was to burst into the room and ask what was going on but, at the same moment, he saw the shape of a man in the glass of the front door. He ran to open it before the man could ring the bell; two was better than one if there was to be a fight.

'Why are you here?' he whispered.

'I have come to see your mother.'

At that moment, the lounge door flew open.

'Run,' screamed Gloria. 'Run, Ahmed, run.'

Ahmed tried to close the front door but Neils was standing in the way. His head slammed between the door and the doorframe and he fell to the ground in pain while Gloria bent over him screaming and crying. The Decorator stepped over her son and shouted to the waiting police to chase him.

By now, Viv was standing on the stairs screaming, adding to the screeching sound of car tires and police sirens.

'Sorry about that young man,' said the Decorator, as he handed Neils two new video games a few days later. 'It was a bit of a cock-up, to put it mildly. I am afraid your father is a member of a terrorist group. We think he became radicalised, quite recently. Sorry lad,' he muttered again, apologetically. 'He got away but we will catch up with him.'

'Cool,' replied Niels.

'I told you to leave it alone,' Gloria shouted, angrily, 'and it is about time you picked up a paintbrush and learnt to help.'

'Not so cool,' laughed the Decorator, who disappeared into the 'rank and file'. Never to be seen again.

*

It was several days before Gloria could bring herself to report Neils missing. It was only after she had received a card, posted in Germany, did she go to the police. It seems he was on his way to Damascus and was happier than he had ever been before.

She had gone to the Iraqi restaurant and heard how Neils had been there. It seems he remembered going there with Ahmed when he was a little boy.

He had arranged for a Decorator to help his mother at a soft price. He had meant well not knowing the man worked for the police. Extremists had contacted and radicalised him before bringing him to his father.

Neils made a wrong choice after living a lie for months.

Gloria put the house up for sale. If either Ahmed or Niels wished to find her and Vivian then they would have to look very hard.

# 'LAUGH-A-PAST'

He could see someone parked in a small Jeep as he approached his house. He frowned for he could not think who it could be though it seemed to be a woman. She took off her scarf and sunglasses letting her blond hair fall onto her shoulders. A woman with a Jeep was not in his address book, not that he knew.

'Jim?'

'Can I help you?'

'Don't you recognise me?'

'Anna' he called, enthusiastically.

She smiled. 'Yes, me.'

'You have a Jeep. Good fun. I must try it out.'

'We could go for a spin like before,' she suggested.

'Yes, we must do that.'

He felt stunned, slightly worried, as they walked into the house. Something between happiness and dread.

Of course, he had realised that after living together for five years she would expect some kind of commitment, perhaps an engagement ring and all that followed. It was not because he did not love her, he was fond of her, fond of her ability to earn a good salary and to keep her apartment incredibly clean and tidy. Not forgetting their uninspired sessions of lovemaking. He was bored and he had thought she felt the same way. He had only done what most of his piers would have done and that was to explore alternative outlets.

He had gone to a popular Bar. Popular because it was known as a stamping ground for lonely females. Girls looking for a bit of fun and with an eye on any possible future husband.

He had hurt Anna and it had seemed to him inevitable that she would leave him or rather chuck him out of her cosy flat. It took her nearly a year before she finally gave up on him.

He had felt relieved when he pulled suitcases off the top of bedroom cupboards and thrown his clothes in as quickly as possible. Anna had stood against the doorframe. He thought she was smiling but he did not want to accept that was possible.

'Here, let me help,' she offered, throwing his clothes back onto the bed and neatly folding them into the suitcase.

'You can come back anytime you want to get the rest of your stuff.'

'I wish it could have been different,' he said, trying to sound sincere.

'Well it wasn't so go and practise your lies on some bimbo. You are a pathological liar. I have even kept a diary noting all the various excuses you have made over the past years. In fact, I have enough to fill a book and that is just what I am going to do. I have been studying you for long enough and I am too busy to have you around me any longer.

Let me know if you can think up any more fantasy stories. I might be able to use them.'

She had helped carry a few plastic bags, mostly with shoes in them, to his Mini car.

'That's the trouble with a car like this. You can't get much in them when you decide to leave your lover.'

He had wanted to hurt her by saying she was hardly what he would call the optimal lover and that his car was a collector's piece.

She had waved as he drove away. He thought she was smiling again. He really did not like her attitude towards him leaving. On the other hand, it was painless. Still, she could have shed a tear or two.

He made a pot of coffee while they talked briefly of the past. Then she kissed him. He recalled the warmth of her body against his, recalled the feel of her, their youthful wild lovemaking.

He had loved Anna with abandonment until he became bored.

He said nothing while she cleared the worktops, rinsed and placed the crockery into the dishwasher. He said nothing as she inspected the contents of his cupboards and refrigerator.

'Humm,' she murmured. 'You haven't learned much over the last years. What stone did you crawl under?'

'I never found the right one.'

'Obviously not,' she replied.

'And you?'

'I found several nesting places. Only storms eventually washed them away.'

He began to laugh. 'I had forgotten your humour.'

'Oh, yes, life is one big joke.'

He grasped her wrist. 'Anna, I am sorry. I made a dreadful mistake.'

'It's never too late to apologise.'

He did not respond to her comment. 'By the way,' he said. 'How did your book go, was it a best seller?'

'Of course, you don't know. I did not make a heap of money but I sold the copyright to Hollywood. They might make a film. Actually, I based my book on you. Remember, I told you I kept a diary. A film director in Hollywood found it explicit and that's what they like.'

'Congratulations. I would like to read it. Maybe it will help to bring back my memory.'

'Is something wrong with your memory?'

'Yes, I am afraid so. I have an unexplainable memory loss. The doctors hope it will slowly return.'

'I am sorry to hear that.'

'I recall living with you.'

'Who said we lived together?'

'We did, didn't we?'

'Yes, we did only I found you so boring I kicked you out. I took a year to do it. I thought you had better first find another ninny so you wouldn't be too lonely.'

'I was never lonely,' he lied.

'If I remember rightly, you could charm the birds out of the trees.'

'Are you still angry with me?'

'I was never angry with you.'

'I was wondering if we went upstairs and made love, then perhaps my memory might return. Just that part of it, you understand.'

She screamed with laughter. 'You haven't changed.'

'Would you love me more if I did?'

'Who says I love you,' she laughed, again.

'We were suited.'

'Your memory must be better than mine.'

'Just for old time's sake, before you leave,' he huddled up to her rather like a small animal seeking security and love.

'Come on, perhaps we could give it another shot,' she suggested.

'A shot in the dark.'

'Perhaps we should leave the light on.'

'Now I remember. You always put the light out.'

'Most people do. I wonder why,' she pondered. 'But I can leave it on if you want to.'

'Your choice,' he replied, pressing his body against hers.

'That brings back memories,' she gasped.

He translated her gasp as consent and imagined how it would be to conquer his lost love. Maybe, he could seduce her to returning to him. To look after him as she had done for five years. He tried to clutch her breasts but she moved aside. He was unsure whether that was by design.

She looked around his bedroom. It was untidy, worn clothes laid on the floor and over a chair. The bed looked as though it had not been washed for weeks or even longer.

'No thanks,' she said. 'I am not that desperate.'

She walked downstairs. 'Let me know if you clean it up.'

'You haven't changed,' he said, angrily.

'You bet I haven't.'

'What about a hotel?'

'Only if you pay.'

'I have a problem with the cash flow. Perhaps you can help me out.'

'Naa, I don't think so. I have to go home to Bernie.'

'Bernie?'

'My husband. He is directing one of those television programmes. You know when they secretly film someone who drops in on their friends from the past. They call it "Laugh-a-Past". I will let you know when it is going to be shown.'

'You can't do that,' he shouted, as she walked out of the front door.

'I think I can,' she yelled back.

'Come back. Do you hear, come back,' he shouted, sounding rather hysterical.

She put her foot down on the accelerator. 'You are not the only one who can lie, darling. You can sit on it until your memory returns.'